*For Eliz
Tka
happy memories of
chapel Hill....
Best wishes*

THE SECRET OF
THE ZEN GARDEN

*from
Sanae Kawaguchi*

SANAE KAWAGUCHI

Copyright © 2013 Sanae Kawaguchi
All rights reserved.
ISBN: 1482025051
ISBN-13: 9781482025057
Library of Congress Control Number: 2013901416
CreateSpace Independent Publishing Platform
North Charleston, South Carolina

All rights reserved. No part of this book may be reproduced or transmitted in any form or by any means, electronic or mechanical, including photocopying, recording, or by any information storage and retrieval system, without permission in writing from the copyright owner.

This is a work of fiction. Names, characters, places or incidents either are the product of the author's imagination or are used fictitiously, and any resemblance to any actual persons, living or dead, events or locales is entirely coincidental.

This book was printed in the United States of America.

DEDICATION

To my dear friends, Michele Ito, Miori Inata, Greg Robinson, HengWee Tan, Itsuo and Elizabeth Kiritani, members of the Weaver Street Gang Dollie Hinch and Bertha Johnson, and so many others whose invaluable help and encouragement made my work possible.

CHAPTER ONE

"But Miyoshi-san, it's been four years now since your husband passed away. You don't have to shut yourself off like this. I understand you're in mourning, but after so long, well, you need to get out of the house sometimes.......Come with me tonight! It is O-Bon after all, and we're supposed to welcome back the spirits of the departed. Surely, no one would criticize you for being out tonight."

Miyoshi smiled wanly, thinking that she would hardly welcome the spirit of her husband. "No, I cannot go out tonight," she replied tersely. As Taiko clucked in a motherly way, Miyoshi quickly added, "You mustn't worry so about me, Taiko-san. It's not that I'm in mourning any more. It's just that I like to be alone to write. I'm used to being alone anyway, and I need the solitude to write. I'm really not shutting myself off."

Mourning for Saburo! The thought made Miyoshi smile. No, she was not mourning for him, a man who had not been much of a husband to her for the twenty years of their marriage.

"But everyone is talking about you," Taiko continued, not to be put off by Miyoshi's protests. It's not natural to live like this, all alone, way up on this mountain, so far from anyone. I mean, if you lived in the village, near us, for instance, no one would say a word about you being alone. But way off here, on this mountain....why, you're like one of those religious hermits or something. How in the world do you get your groceries and other supplies....?"

Miyoshi fidgeted uneasily. She had always been a shy person and the attention she was getting from Saburo's relations in the village made her acutely nervous. Perhaps it had been a mistake choosing a place so close to Saburo's family village. She had not meant to be close to them, but she remembered once, when Saburo brought her to see the famous house on the mountain, she had been so taken by the beauty of the house, the famous garden and the spectacular view of the mountains. It was known to be a fine example of Japanese farmhouse architecture, and she had been strangely drawn to the place, as if she had known it before.

"Oh, I love this place! I wish I could live here!" she had exclaimed to Saburo. But he had just laughed at her.

"Who would think of living in such a place, so far away from anything? That's just like you to want something so strange," he snorted, shaking his head in exasperation.

After Saburo's death four years ago, when she found the house was for sale at a very reasonable price, she had impulsively bought it. There was only a dirt road leading to the place, and it was enough of a climb from the village to make it less accessible. A greengrocer in the village had agreed to make regular deliveries of whatever she needed, so that she could stay away from the village and all of Saburo's relatives. In the beginning, Saburo's family had not bothered much with her, but when she began to acquire some fame, they began to come around more frequently. It made her uneasy, and she wanted even more to burrow into her secluded glen.

Taiko's voice brought Miyoshi out of her musing.

"And it's not only that, it's the way this place looks…" Taiko gestured to the weed grown garden. "Why, just see how rundown it's become. You know, old Mr. Hasegawa, who built this house, was a fanatic about the place. It was even featured in a magazine as a fine example of Japanese architecture. People came from far away just to see this place. The garden, especially, was famous. Now look! It looks like it hasn't been touched in years!"

Miyoshi turned her gaze to the overgrown yard, and felt a pang of guilt. She had remembered the garden in the days of old Mr. Hasegawa. After Saburo first showed her the place, she had come to it several times on her own because she so enjoyed the garden and the views of the mountain. When she heard that it had been empty for some time and no one seemed to want it, she had put in a bid to buy it. At the time, she did not think about Saburo's relatives living in the village nearby. It seemed a wonderful opportunity to live in such a beautiful place and the price was so reasonable. The garden was why she had loved it so in the first place, and now, she realized, she had paid no attention to it in the four years she had been living in the house. For once, she really looked at it. It surprised her to see how neglected it looked. She realized she had not really looked at it since she first bought the house after her husband's death. At that time, she had only wanted to escape the unexpectedly ardent attention from the readers of her first enormously successful novel. Miyoshi was surprised by the popularity of the book, especially among young women. She had written the book after Saburo's death as a way of comforting herself, not for losing Saburo so much as for the loss she felt of all the romantic hopes and dreams she had had about her marriage when she first married Saburo. Somehow her romantic yearnings had struck a responsive chord among young women and she had become an overnight celebrity.

Being naturally shy and reclusive, she had run off in desperation to Saburo's family village, way off in the mountains of the Minami Alps, far enough away from Tokyo to escape prying eyes and nosy journalists. The house had looked old and neglected, but the isolated location had immediately appealed to her. At the time, she had not really paid much attention to the garden or the house, except for the areas she used every day. She had given the garden a cursory glance, filing in her mind a reminder to find someone to fix the garden. Then, thoughts of the garden receded from the pressure of her work, which took precedence and kept her too busy to think of anything else. Her publisher, after the success of her first book, urged her to quickly turn out another book, and then a third. And now she was trying to complete the fourth before the deadline they had set.

"Yes, I had thought to make it into a proper garden," Miyoshi interrupted Taiko, who would have gone on forever about the run down condition of the garden. "I thought maybe a Zen garden, perhaps, a place of quiet contemplation…."

Taiko's round cheerful face lit up immediately. "Why, I know just the one to do it! My nephew! He's at loose ends now. He was studying to be a Zen priest, you know. But he changed his mind. He'd been studying for eight years and then, just suddenly, he said the priesthood was not for him. Imagine that? Now he's just hanging around his mother's house and doing odd jobs here and there. His mother, that's my sister, Misae, you remember her….is quite worried about him. He's already thirty years old. He should be thinking of settling down, finding a good job, getting married….it would be difficult, though, to find a wife for him unless he had a job of some kind…….But he doesn't listen to anything his mother says. Young people now days…." Taiko sighed

Taiko seemed set on having a nice, long chat and Miyoshi was getting impatient. Taiko quickly interjected.

"Oh, but he's a very hard worker. If he has something to do, he puts himself into it wholeheartedly. He's not a bit lazy! And he doesn't just lie around drinking beer, or hanging out at Pachinko parlors….no, no, he's a good boy………"

"Yes, perhaps it would be a good idea to fix the garden," Miyoshi broke in quickly. Her mind was on her work and she was only half-listening, pacifying Taiko to bring the visit to an end. She had promised her publisher she would be finished with her current novel in two weeks, but it was proving to be harder to resolve the ending than she had imagined. She had always had an intense concentration that had enabled her to write three novels in the years since her husband's death. It was as if his death had opened a floodgate and words had gushed forth in an unchecked spate.

Lately, however, she had noticed a restlessness about her, a tendency for her mind to wander. She frowned in annoyance at this lack of concentration on her work.

Taiko had been searching Miyoshi's face to see how she should proceed to implement her latest plan. She misread the frown on Miyoshi's face. Miyoshi is probably annoyed at the cost of fixing the garden, she surmised. She thought it very miserly of her to think about money, when everyone knew she was so rich from her books – and what did she have to spend it on, anyway? A bit critically, she added, "Oh, don't worry, you won't have to pay Tadao very much since he's not a professional gardener. But he worked in the garden at the Zen monastery and he's not afraid of hard work.

You are a successful writer, after all, and should live like one. Your books are selling well, so you're doing all right for yourself," she said, a bit reproachfully.

"Oh, no….it's not the money!" Miyoshi answered quickly "Of course I would pay to have the garden done. And I would pay him as much as any gardener. But it's ….well….it's a matter of the time. I would like to do the garden to suit me, and I wouldn't be able to do it for awhile…"

"Leave it to me", Taiko said briskly, accepting no excuses. Her mind was already busy sorting out the possibilities. Taiko's round face beamed with pleasure. She was happiest when she was making "arrangements" for others, whether it was something as important as the right school for her sons, or as trivial as a new hair ornament, and especially if it was something as serious as finding a suitable match for someone. She had been the nakodo – matchmaker- for a number of village couples. This was, however, a different kind of match – the right person for the right job. But she could handle this. Empowered now with a mission, she gathered herself together, jammed her calloused feet into her sturdy shoes, so much in a hurry that the heels were squashed down as she hurried out the door. She bustled off down the dirt road as if a swarm of gnats were buzzing around her.

Miyoshi sat for along time gazing at the garden after Taiko left. Idly, she put the tea things back on a tray to take to the kitchen. Fragmented, absent thoughts wafted idly, finding no place to light. The heat and humidity of the July day had made her languid and she was reluctant to get back to her desk. A faint mist softened the outline of the mountains surrounding the glen. There was not even a hint of a breeze to clear the veil that hung over the trees. The rasping of cicadas grated on her mind and images of Saburo, whom she had not thought of for years, prodded her memory. Saburo, so handsome at twenty-five, with a wicked gleam in his eyes that made her feel faint when she first met him. Saburo, at thirty-five, driven by his job, often too tired or bored to be moved by desire at the sight of her. Saburo at forty-five, eyes dulled by whiskey, for he was drinking constantly by then. It was what salarymen had to do to keep up with their coworkers. He lived with the nagging feeling that life had passed him by. The brash confidence of his youth was gone, replaced by a surly discontent that life had not treated him fairly. He had masked his fears with drink and harsh criticism of Miyoshi. She had endured it all, expecting this as her lot in life, no different from many Japanese wives. Her failure to produce a child, she told herself, was why he was so angry, so disappointed in her. For her failure, she must endure his bad temper.

When things got too bad, Miyoshi would retire to her desk, putting her thoughts in a journal. Having been a painfully shy person all her life, she had no one to confide in, so her journal became her way to escape. Gradually, her escape also became an avid interest in her life. She began to write about things that caught her eye, descriptions of people, observing them and imagining the lives they led. But she carefully kept this to herself. The outer Miyoshi was a proper, quiet, serious and hard-working wife, obedient to her husband's wishes. As a result, she was greatly admired by the relatives and neighbors who considered her a paragon, the embodiment of the Japanese feminine ideal.

"Oh, what a good wife they think I am!" she had written in her journal one day after five years of marriage. "But if people could see what I am really thinking! If they knew of my longings, of how I yearn to have Saburo make love to me as eagerly as he had when we first married….how my body aches for him…how it hurts that he does not want me any more! Yet how can I tell him how I feel? Sometimes I want to scream at him when he scolds me, but I force a smile and quietly serve his beer. Sometimes, even now, I feel wanton like the lowest prostitute, but I primly fasten my yukata and lie still by his side."

Gradually, Miyoshi guessed that many of the nights Saburo stayed out late "on business" were spent with other women. Saburo was attractive to women, even in his later years. It was nothing she could prove, or even speak to Saburo about. At first, it had been agony to endure the images she conjured in her mind. Her active imagination had exaggerated Saburo's sexual conquests, for the truth was not nearly as exciting or romantic as she imagined. His partners were bar women or prostitutes and he was often too drunk to perform. Yet, the jealousy she felt had shocked her with the intensity of her emotion. The jealousy and rage – did this prove she really loved him so much, she thought, that she should be filled with such intense pain at the thought of Saburo lying in another woman's arms?

But the traditional restraints she had learned from childhood pressed down on her with the weight of centuries of indoctrination. She scolded herself. Didn't she know that all men were like that? It didn't mean anything. It was just something that women had to endure. Being a good Japanese meant enduring, accepting what cannot be helped and making the best of things.

Being a respectable housewife, there was no one Miyoshi could talk to about such personal matters. Her journal was her confidante, but it could offer her no advice. It only helped a little to assuage the pain.

Saburo's death of a heart attack at such an early age had been a shock to her, but the loneliness she had known for most of her life had prepared her well for widowhood. Then, her writing had taken up all of her time and interest. The enormous creative flow had kept thoughts of her deep inner life safely hidden. In her books, she dwelt on the dreamy, romantic fantasies of young girls. In this way, she could keep her private thoughts safely locked away. She had not allowed herself the luxury of such egocentric thoughts, any more than she allowed herself to spend money that now flowed in. Now that she could afford things for herself, it was as if the fear of Saburo's criticism still lingered, and she hesitated to get anything for her own pleasure. It was fortunate that she had simple tastes and no desire for ostentatious things.

Miyoshi had a Spartan childhood. She had been born in 1930, when Japan was coming into its time of military conquests in Asia. All of Japan's resources had gone into the war. The entire country was stretched to the limits of their productivity for the war effort. Then, the terrible time of the American bombardment and eventual defeat, put even more privations on the populace. After the War, everyone in Japan was struggling only to survive each day.

Her natural shyness as a child, and then her long isolation as Saburo's wife, did not prepare her for the success of her first book. It had been a terrifying intrusion into her very private existence. She had fled to the isolated glen to escape the attention her success had brought. She felt safe in her little glen, with only the narrow dirt road for access and separated by a mountain from the village below. It was difficult enough to reach to keep most people away. She didn't miss people – she had always felt different from other people and never had any real friends. However, as reading was her greatest pleasure, she allowed herself her one luxury of buying as many books as she liked.

Then, too, her great enjoyment in the beauty of nature gave her peace and contentment. The constantly changing view as each season waxed and waned, the cozy warmth of her comfortable house – with so much to please her in her surroundings and with so much to occupy her mind, she did not miss the company of people.

Taiko's conversation made her think of the garden again. She looked at the weed-choked yard, the thick misshapen trees, and the garden gate askew. Where once there had been a trickling stream, now only rocks lay strewn about. There was only a faint trace of the former beauty of the garden. Gardens need tender, caring hands, constantly tending it, she thought. But she had not cared for anything or anyone except her books for the past four years. And what did she have to show for it...? The garden seemed to be a reflection of her life, gently reproaching her.

"Yes, it would be nice to have a Zen garden. It might even help me with my work, to have a place to pull my thoughts together....yes....a quiet place of contemplation....."

Pleased with the thought, Miyoshi's lips softened with a hint of sensuality that would have surprised her if she had seen it.

CHAPTER TWO

Taiko wasted little time making arrangements to have her nephew, Tadao, work on Miyoshi's garden. She did not ask Tadao directly, however, for directness was not the proper Japanese way. Instead, she took Tadao's mother aside that evening when they all went to the cemetery to light the O-Bon fires.

As they walked along the village streets, people were lighting small fires at the entry to their homes to guide the spirits of the dead back home. Taiko and Tadao's mother, Misae, had tiny bundles of firewood to make the fires at the gravesites, and sticks of incense, which they would light at each of the relatives' graves. The warm, humid night air kept the smoke hovering over the village in a soft cloud. Everywhere, they ran into relatives and friends and it became a busy time of gossiping, seeing old friends, and catching up on the latest news, as they lit incense and bowed in prayer at each stop. Whole families had turned out most dressed in summer yukatas. Small boys wore traditional checked patterns while young girls in bright colors and patterns added gaiety to the scene. It was a friendly occasion, as well as a time to remember the deceased with fond memories. O-Bon gave a person a sense of one's own family history and one's place in it, and as such, it was a very important holiday in Japan. People living away from their home villages would make a trip home just for the occasion.

At the last gravesite, Taiko finally had a chance to take Misae aside and talk to her privately. The crowds had thinned out and they took a moment to rest on a bench at the edge of the cemetery. Taiko let out a sigh as she fussed with the bundle she was carrying, and made sure Misae was paying attention.

"I tried to get Miyoshi-san to come tonight," said Taiko, "but she wouldn't. It's really too sad, the way she shuts herself off," Taiko added sadly, but with a hint of criticism in her voice.

Misae nodded in perfect agreement. "Miyoshi-san was always a bit strange…"

"Well, it's not good for her," said Taiko. "And it doesn't reflect well on us, either. After all, Saburo was our cousin and she has no other family."

"No, I believe she has an older sister somewhere…. up north…in Iwate, I believe. I heard her sister was married to some rich man, very important around there. But the sisters are not very close," added Misae.

"Anyway," Taiko cut in, annoyed at being put off her line of approach. "That's neither here nor there. We are Miyoshi-san's family and she lives here. And it looks bad the way she lives. Her place looks so shabby, so run-down. Have you seen it…? No, I guess you haven't …Well, her garden is a mess, all overgrown. You remember how old Mr. Hasegawa used to take such pride in his garden. Oh, my, if he could see it now! And it isn't a question of money, either. You know she can afford to live well."

"Of course," agreed Misae, "everyone knows her books are selling well. She must be quite well off. And, of course, I imagine Saburo left her provided for…."

"Well, when I told her about the garden, Miyoshi-san said she wanted some kind of a Zen garden. So, well, I suggested she get Tadao to fix her garden for her. He should certainly know about such things, working at that Zen monastery for so long…..and they were famous for their gardens, too."

"Tadao….hmmm," Misae frowned. "He's off fishing tonight. He says the fish better look out because he is getting serious about fishing!" Misae laughed, remembering Tadao's comical face as he set off that evening. No matter what he did, he was her favorite and he could always make her laugh. "I don't think that means he's serious about being a fisherman, though," Misae sighed. "He's got his mind set on catching the 'big one'. But he gets no money for that kind of fishing. I guess if Miyoshi-san can pay him to do her garden, that's at least a decent job. I'll talk to him about it."

"Good," said Taiko, well pleased with her night's work.

When his mother talked to Tadao, he accepted the job cheerfully, since he had no other thing to do. In fact, he was usually very cheerful, and though this made his constant presence a pleasure to Misae, she often worried that he was not serious enough about anything. True, he did spend a lot of his time reading, not hanging around bars or coffee houses or pachinko parlors like some young men. He was a good boy, Misae told herself, so why did he worry her so? He had always been a bit different from his older brothers, but perhaps it was because he had been sickly as a child and she had kept him at home much of the time. He became her special child, if only because he required so much attention. Even now, though he was healthy enough, he had a deceptively frail appearance. His tall, thin frame looked gangly and awkward, as if he had never overcome that sudden spurt of growth in his teens.

When Tadao announced, eight years ago, that he wanted to study to be a Zen priest, Misae had been astonished. Yet she was also pleased that he was finally so serious about something. Every Japanese male should have a profession, something that established his place in the community. Young men who hung about doing nothing were looked on with contempt. Misae and her husband gave Tadao their whole-hearted approval and support. After all, their ambitions had been fulfilled with two sons successfully employed in government service. They could let one son, at least, do whatever he pleased – as long as it was respectable.

So it had been upsetting to his parents when Tadao came home, with no further talk of being a priest. No real explanation. "It just wasn't for me," was all he would say. But even now, Misae knew, he often sat zazen in his room late at night. Though he sat in a darkened room, she could see his straight back outlined against the pale moonlight, absolutely still. She could feel a power emanating from that stillness, a stillness that he could maintain for hours.

This son was a paradox to her. So utterly serious as he sat zazen, yet so full of silly antics just to make Misae laugh. So at ease with almost anyone, yet preferring to spend most of his time alone. So philosophical in his choice of reading materials, yet he enjoyed watching the most inane and trivial comedy on TV. So attentive to her, but if she tried to "mother" him, he would resist stubbornly, or become distant and push her away.

"I will never understand this child," Misae confided to her husband. "Maybe he's been enchanted by some kind of spirit," she laughed.

"Nonsense. Tadao needs a wife, that's all," said Misae's husband. "That will settle him down."

"But who would marry him, a young man with no job, no prospects? We're not a rich family, after all, not exactly the kind some nice girl would be attracted to...."

"What do you mean?" her husband was offended, for though he was now retired, he considered himself to have done well as a minor government official. But Misae went on, ignoring him, intent on her own thoughts. "No, he has to find some kind of job or he'll never get a wife." Her husband agreed reluctantly, though Misae did not hear him.

Perhaps, Misae thought hopefully, this job for Miyoshi-san will be a good beginning. One good thing about Tadao was that he showed no reluctance to do hard work, she thought with satisfaction. Once he found a place for himself, she was sure, he would do every bit as well as his brothers.

CHAPTER THREE

The next day, Tadao made his way up the narrow, stony lane to the small glen where Miyoshi's house nestled in the embrace of some low mountains. It was a warm day, the cicadas were whirring noisily in the bamboo groves. The air was still, with a soft humidness coming from the dewy grass. It was not an easy climb, but Tadao was used to climbing these mountains, as he had grown up exploring them since childhood. He enjoyed these Southern Alps, as it was called, in all its seasons and moods. He was always happy when he was away from crowds or signs of human habitation. And, as always when he was outdoors, he gave himself up to the simple pleasure he found in nature. The warm sun felt good on his back, and he even enjoyed the beads of sweat that occasionally dripped into his eyes as he climbed the mountain. His mind was in a kind of nothingness, drifting from time to time to alight on the beauty around him, the sights, sounds, smells, tastes of this warm, sunny day. The melons he carried as a gift from his mother were a light burden. Even a heavy burden would not have bothered him much, inured as he was after eight years at the monastery, to hard physical work. Though he looked frail, he had honed his body with work, and enjoyed pushing himself to test his limits.

As he neared Miyoshi's house, he had a brief curiosity about this woman he was to work for. Aunt Miyoshi, she with the mannish name, was known to him by reports only. He heard stories about her when the family gathered, but he had never met her before. She had been living in Tokyo with Saburo all those years, with only rare visits to their village. Though she had moved to their area four years ago, he had been at the monastery, and so far had never met her. His family saw little of her, as she almost never went down into the village. She had her groceries and other needs provided by a merchant in the village who delivered what she needed once a week. She was known to everyone as a recluse who did not welcome attention from anyone. Because she had achieved a kind of celebrity, the family was somewhat in awe of her. Still, the general feeling about her was that "Miyoshi-san is a bit strange." Knowing so little about her, Tadao pictured a rather prim, gaunt old woman, looking perhaps, like one of the stern monks at the monastery.

He did not see the house until he was almost upon it. The weather worn wood and the old-fashioned thatched roof bleached into the colors of the surrounding mountains. Though it looked old and somewhat run-down, it had been thoughtfully and sensitively designed to create a beautiful harmony with its surroundings. It nestled softly in a fold of the mountains, seeming to be a natural part of the glen. The beauty was not lost on Tadao. He nodded to himself in appreciation and deference to the builder of the house.

Pushing aside the entrance gate, he looked around for some sign of Miyoshi.

"Obasan...?" Tadao called, as he knocked on her door, for there was no bell in sight. "Excuse me for disturbing you like this..." he began.

"Oh, no, not at all!" said Miyoshi, appearing a bit flustered, at the entryway. When she saw him, she smiled to herself, for he had an odd look about him. Terribly awkward, and he seems very shy, rather like a crane, she thought, all gangly arms and long spindly legs. She almost expected a hoarse crane-like rasp from his long throat and was delighted with the unexpectedly low and melodious sound of his voice.

"Um…er…excuse me…" he repeated, startled by her appearance.

Miyoshi flashed him a welcoming smile to put him at ease.

"Your mother called and told me you would be coming today. Please do come in," she said, offering him a pair of house slippers.

Her looks and warm manner threw him off completely. Not the stern old monk, not a ragged looking hermit, but a slender, graceful woman of a rather indeterminate age. Tadao fumbled with his shoes and almost tripped on the step up, still recovering from his surprise at the sight of this aunt's appearance. Outwardly, she seemed normally healthy, her skin was youthful, with no wrinkles at all, and her hair had no trace of gray. It was pulled back into one long braid which somehow made her look young and vulnerable. She had a childlike innocence about her, but there was also an indescribable air about her, one he might have recognized as a latent sensuality if he had been more experienced and worldly. No, she certainly bore no resemblance to that crusty old monk!

Miyoshi's friendly manner put Tadao immediately at ease. He accepted a cup of tea and rice crackers as they talked. Surprisingly, conversation came easily for both of them. Miyoshi did not feel her usual shyness, possibly because he was a relative, and he was so young.

In fact, she felt strangely at ease with him, as if she had known him for a long time. As for Tadao, who was not, by nature, a gregarious person, it seemed perfectly natural to chat with Miyoshi. Perhaps he knew her in some other lifetime, he thought. He realized later that he had talked more easily with Miyoshi than he had ever talked to anyone else outside his own family – and not even so easily with them. It was like talking to an old childhood friend that he had not seen in many years. Soon he found himself telling her about his life at the monastery, his feeling for nature that came from working in the monastery garden.

Miyoshi had always been a good listener, even to Saburo. Now that she was enjoying what Tadao had to say, she listened more intently. She could see that Tadao had the same feeling for nature, an empathy with her that predicted they would work well together, and she felt a warm glow of anticipation.

"I'm almost ashamed to show you this garden," she said at last, when there was finally a lull in the conversation.

"Mother said you wanted a Zen garden…maybe you could tell me what you mean…?"

"I don't know…exactly….just a place of quiet contemplation…rocks, moss, a few shrubs, something quite simple, really."

"Ummmm…." Tadao gazed at the garden for a while but no thoughts came to mind.

"Well, of course it is impossible to imagine now, with all those weeds…" he said at last. "I guess I'll have to clear it out first to see what is there."

"Yes, of course. There's a tool shed next to the garage. Here, let me show you," said Miyoshi, leading the way. "And if there is anything you need, please just get it and I will pay for it."

Somehow they even managed the awkward discussion of payment for Tadao's work with a minimum of discomfort, partly because Tadao wanted so modest a sum and Miyoshi was willing to pay a generous one. A compromise was easily reached.

"I'll start clearing up a bit right now, then," said Tadao, unraveling his gangly legs and straightening up. His face lit up with a cheerful grin, eager to get started.

Miyoshi sent him on his way, pleased with their interview. She was sure he would understand exactly what she wanted for her garden. Her ease with him surprised her.

Being a solitary person, Miyoshi did not usually give her trust so easily, but somehow she was confident this strange-looking young man would do a good job. She set her mind to rest and went back to her writing. She managed to concentrate on her work, yet occasionally, her attention was caught by the unfamiliar sound of Tadao's activities, or by a glimpse of his gangly form wrestling with armloads of weeds. She smiled at the sight of him and it came to her mind that he was strangely graceful as he moved.

CHAPTER FOUR

Tadao arrived early every morning, often before Miyoshi was up. She was in the habit of working late into the night. It seemed the best time for the isolation and concentration she needed for her work when she first started to write and the habit still persisted in spite of the isolation the glen provided. Night seemed warm and friendly – daytime was for enjoying nature, or doing housework, or running errands. So the habits she had acquired during her years in Tokyo persisted even in the undisturbed quiet of the glen.

By the time she had her breakfast, Tadao was ready for a morning break and a cup of tea. They easily fell into sharing this time together. The rapport they had established on their first meeting continued and before long, they began to feel familiar and comfortable in each other's company. Miyoshi liked Tadao's light banter, which could turn swiftly into a sensitive observance of some aspect of nature. These sudden changes amused her, or challenged her to see things from a new perspective. She found that Tadao had not so much a facile, surface intellect, but a deep intuitive understanding that cut through to the heart of things, so that she was often astonished at the deep levels she uncovered in him.

Looking at him one day as he worked, long and intently for the first time, Miyoshi had a shock. When she had first seen him, she had not considered him handsome, certainly not in the film star way Saburo had been at that age, but now, the intensity of his expression, the mobility of his features, the way his eyes crinkled with delight, made his face a most interesting landscape.

"How different he is from Saburo," she thought, and she did not mean only his looks. Saburo had been a more two-dimensional man, not terribly complicated. At least, he never revealed any complexity of character to her. After the first few weeks of their marriage, she seldom saw him, for he worked long hours. Weekends were often spent with his friends or co-workers on the golf course, or on some outing which did not include wives. Their conversations, when she waited up for him late at night, were usually desultory, mundane, concerned only with household matters.

In the first year, Miyoshi had not minded the lack of conversation for Saburo's sexual appetite had awakened her own sensuality and there was no need for conversation. But as work and Saburo's outside activities lessened his demand for her, she began to long for some more intimacy in their conversations. Though she tried to engage him in conversation, he merely seemed annoyed.

"I'm tired," he would mutter and go straight to bed. Saburo had never taken any notice of her needs. If they had had a child that would have become the focus of her life and she would not notice the lack of intimacy with Saburo. Unfortunately, she had never been able to conceive, and somehow, Saburo seemed to hold that against her. She knew that men often divorced wives who were barren, and she appreciated that Saburo had never mentioned divorce. In her gratitude, she felt she had no right to complain about any lack of attention from Saburo. She tried even harder to be a good wife.

After years of controlled and polite talk with her husband, and her long self-imposed isolation, it was a treat for Miyoshi to be able to talk openly with someone. She came to look forward eagerly to her morning talks with Tadao. When her book was finally finished, she decided to put off any more writing for a while and give herself some time off to work with Tadao on the garden. He would not let her do any heavy work, but she enjoyed digging in the soil. She liked the musky smell of the damp earth, the bitter tang of the weeds. She liked the way her muscles responded to the work she now demanded of them. It was a much-needed antidote to the purely mental work she had been doing and she attacked the garden work with zest and vigor.

As the days passed, there was a noticeable change in Miyoshi. She, herself, did not notice particularly the gradual softening of her features, the faint glow on her skin, or the sparkle in her eyes. Only someone who knew her intimately might see the change. Miyoshi only knew that she felt better than she had in a long time. She attributed it to being outdoors, getting healthy exercise. She realized with wonder, that all her senses seemed sharpened, so that she was acutely aware of the scenery around her. She had always enjoyed her views of the mountain, but had she ever really noticed it before? Did she see the variations of color as the mountains faded away? Did the cedars always have such a pungent smell? Did the hydrangea bush have such an astringent odor? Did the birds always trill so each morning by her window? She noticed the ugiusu bird, and the changes in his call as the season progressed. Funny, she had never noticed the dove cote next to the tool shed….nor heard the cooing of the doves. Why did the grass look so green, and smell so musty? And was the sky always so vivid a blue, the mountains so softly lavender….? She felt as if she were awakening from a long and heavy sleep, a gentle awakening, a languorous and sensuous awareness creeping slowly through her body.

At first she put the change to the release from the tension of working on her books. It was the first real break she had taken for years; the first time to do only what she wanted to do, without wifely duties or publishing deadlines. She felt giddy and childish at times and Tadao seemed to sense and attune himself to her mood.

She and Tadao cornered a lizard in the garden one day and chased it pell mell over rocks, around bushes and scrambling through the trees until they both collapsed in a fit of laughter. She could not remember the last time she had laughed so hard.

Yet Tadao had his serious side, too. One day, after telling her about his life in the monastery, he taught her how to sit zazen. She found it terribly difficult, but he got her properly positioned on a cushion so that her body was in perfect balance and alignment. This made the physical part manageable, but her mind was impossible to control. To concentrate only on her breathing was beyond her ability and her busy mind kept filling up with a wild assortment of images and thoughts. She was determined to stick to it, however, so every morning, she sat very still, gazing down at the tatami mat, trying to empty her mind. Tadao tiptoed around and made the morning tea for them, waiting patiently until she was ready.

Making the morning tea turned into making breakfast for her, a good nourishing breakfast of Tadao's own devising. He was interested in the healing quality of certain herbs and the health values of various foods from his days at the monastery. There had been a monk there who grew all sorts of herbs and Tadao had learned much from him. He convinced Miyoshi to put in an herb garden, and to grow some other vegetables as well. He said natural, untreated food was best for the body. He made brown rice mixed with millet and buckwheat, or with barley and job's tears. Miyoshi liked the things he made and the more she enjoyed it, the more he tried new dishes to please her.

"You are spoiling me," she protested one day, but Tadao only grinned and said he enjoyed cooking. Miyoshi could not remember the last time anyone had cooked for her, cosseted her, or served her – probably not since she was a toddler. At first, she was flustered by his attentions, but he made it seem so natural and so much fun for him, that she did not have the heart to spoil his pleasure.

Tadao was always exploring the area around the house, looking for plants that might be interesting for her garden. There were a few loquat trees at the foot of the mountain and one day, Miyoshi and Tadao made an excursion to gather loquat leaves. Tadao said loquats had many healing qualities and he promised to make her a special extraction to use when she had any aches or pains.

"Oh, yes...at my age, doing all that gardening does make me ache!" she laughed.

"It's not your age – everyone has aches and pains," he protested, for suddenly he found he did not like to think of her as old.

They scrambled through the heavy brush to get to the leaves and Miyoshi laughed as Tadao climbed agilely up a tree to gather some leaves. He said the dark, older leaves were the best, for they had absorbed a lot of healing power. As he picked, he hung suspended from a branch, making monkey sounds to get her attention. She found in his silly antics, an uncanny understanding of the creature he mimicked, as if he had actually become a monkey, as if he understood on some primal level how a monkey actually feels. He had a natural affinity for animals of any kind. When he did an awkward crane dance for her one day, he again seemed to know instinctively how a crane would move. His gawky movements expressed the strange grace of the bird perfectly.

After a few weeks, the weeds and brush had been cleared away. Miyoshi could finally see the dimensions of her garden.

"I think I'd like the sound of water here....soft, muted..." she said.

"There's a spring near the loquat trees. Maybe we could divert that water to come through here...that is, if the owner of that land agrees," he added.

"The owner says 'yes'," she replied, and was pleased to catch the surprised look on his face. "Oh, yes," she added, in mock seriousness," I am a woman of property so please have proper respect!"

He kowtowed obsequiously, until she stopped him with a nudge and a burst of disrespectful laughter.

Such were the childish games they played, the innocent joy they found in each other's company. Perhaps because he was so much younger, there was not the usual inhibition that existed between the sexes. And since she had never had a child, he seemed a delightful child to her, or so she told herself. On his part, he looked on her as the kind of friend he had never had – fun loving, adventurous, attentive, and appreciative – and for the first time in his life, someone he could really talk to.

The work on the garden did not go on every day; there were many times when they just sat and talked, or found other diversions that had nothing to do with the garden. He made small improvements on her house, mending a wall here, fixing the floor there, and making the kitchen windows wider so she could have a better view of the mountains.

He amazed her with his range of abilities and knowledge. He wove baskets for her from reeds he found along the stream. He cut bamboo and made vases for her. He collected stones from the streambed for her front entry hall. And all he did, he did with a sunny good humor that filled Miyoshi's house and her heart with joy.

One day he told her about the monastery and why he had left.

"I realized one day, I didn't have the dedication. If I were going to be a priest, a real Roshi, I would have to be completely devoted. But I did not have that kind of devotion. I guess I'm not serious enough. That's what my parents always say. I think I'm serious enough. But I wanted other things, too. Maybe I'm just too lazy," he laughed ruefully.

"What do you want to do, then?" she asked.

"I don't know. Right now, I feel very confused, as if I've lost my way. I thought for many years that I knew what I wanted, that if I believed, if I practiced meditation earnestly, the right way, I would find a place for me. I wanted to find enlightenment, like the Buddha. But the head priest told me that the very wanting to find enlightenment was desire, that I had to free myself from ALL desire, including the desire for enlightenment. I didn't think I could do that. Now, I am not sure….now, I think I am nothing…. sometimes…"

Miyoshi was deeply moved. She felt a great tenderness and compassion for him, for she could feel his pain. It reached out to the deep pain she had kept hidden inside her for so many years. She, too, had thought of herself as nothing, a mere shadow of Saburo, moving as a puppet to his will. Yet, because this was the traditional role of the Japanese woman, Miyoshi had not allowed herself to resent her subservient position. Tadao's confession brought her own feelings welling up, coming at last to the surface of her consciousness.

Gently, she took his hand and held it quietly. They said not a word, but sat for along time like that, looking vaguely at the mist-covered mountains. Though they said nothing, their communion of grief had forged a bond between them.

CHAPTER FIVE

The next day, the skies appeared dark and threatening. The typhoon season was now on them and the days would be unpredictable. Miyoshi looked anxiously at the sky, thinking Tadao would not come, though they had talked of digging a ditch that day to divert the spring. She felt a pang of disappointment at the thought that he might not come. She busied herself making breakfast, but thoughts of Tadao, remembrances of the breakfasts he had made so especially for her, made her solitary tray seem suddenly terribly lonely. The depth of her feeling surprised her and she realized that she had come to depend on his presence to frame the mood of the day.

    Tadao had been unnaturally quiet when he left the day before. Miyoshi wondered if she had embarrassed him by holding his hand. Touching was not the usual and proper Japanese way – even when Miyoshi had not seen her parents for many years, she only bowed when she greeted them. She could not remember when anyone had touched her, other than Saburo when he had needed her body. Yet when she had held Tadao's hand, it had seemed the most natural thing to do.

But he arrived, a bit later than usual, for he had brought a special surprise for her. He grinned broadly as he heaved a heavy wheelbarrow up the path to the house.

"Tadao-san!" she exclaimed, delight and excitement lighting up her eyes, but quickly clouded by concern for the heavy load he was carrying. He was staggering and weaving along the path.

He set the wheelbarrow down beside her and mopped his face with a towel he untied from his forehead.

"It's something for the garden," he said, with a shy, tentative grin.

"What is it…?" Miyoshi was puzzled, for she could see only some rocks laid out in the barrow.

"Wait – you'll see," he said, unloading the rocks and carrying them into the garden.

She watched eagerly as he set the rocks carefully into place. Now she could see they were not plain rocks, but had been artfully worked into a form.

"Oh! How wonderful! It's a garden lantern! But it's a most unusual lantern….where did you find it?" she asked.

"I made it, from rocks I found along the stream. I had my stonemason friend make some alterations to fit my design, but basically, it's just the natural rocks. I thought it would fit the garden better than the usual molded concrete lantern."

"Oh, it is perfect! It has such….a…harmony, such perfect balance. Oh, Tadao-san, it is a beautiful lantern! I like it very much!"

Tadao glowed with pleasure at her praise and her obvious delight. It was such a joy for him to do things for her, for she always appreciated the things he did. It made him want to do more, to outdo himself, just to see the look on her face.

For Miyoshi, Tadao's many gifts, his attentions, all the things he did for her, were overwhelming. Born as she was in the hard times before, during and the end of the war, life had been a fragile and difficult thing for many years. Her parents could never give her anything, for, like everyone else in Japan in those years, it was all they could do to just survive from day to day. Everyone worked long hours to eke out a mere subsistence. Miyoshi grew up never expecting anything for herself. Nor had Saburo, in all their years of marriage, ever given her a gift.

Tadao, on the other hand, was always doing things for her. Not only in his work on the garden and around the house, which he considered part of his job, but also in the beautiful things he made. He gave her such delight in so many ways. This lantern, however, exceeded anything he had done before. It was a very special gift, a work of art, so beautifully worked that it looked artless. Tears filled her eyes and words would not come from her throat. He, too, stood awkwardly, touched by her tears, yet unable to respond.

"Come," she said at last, "let us sit on the veranda and have a cup of tea so we can look at this lantern," and without thinking, she again took his hand to lead him to the house.

"Tadao-san," she said, as they sat sipping their tea, "You're such a fine artist. Not only the lantern, which is really a work of art, but all the things you have made for me – the baskets, the bamboo vases – you have a natural talent."

"Oh, that's just traditional craft work. I just do it for fun. I'm not really serious about it. It's not like being an artist," he said, a bit embarrassed by her praise.

"Perhaps that is the best kind of art, the thing that is done for the joy of doing."

"It's nothing, really. I'm not anything at all – just fooling around…."

"Tadao-san, it is NOT a nothing! You are not a nothing. You are someone very unique, a person with a true heart of an artist. That's a very rare gift. I write books and some say they are good, but I never think of myself as any kind of artist. My books are light entertainment, not art.

But the things you make have a special quality that....that can't be defined by words. I say that is art, that indefinable something that makes a thing unique."

He looked at her, confused by her words, troubled by them, yet, strangely, comforted, too. He watched her silently as she poured tea, enjoying the grace of her movements. At that moment, there was a soft halo of light around her face as the sun broke through the clouds. Suddenly, her beauty caught his breath. Until then, he had not thought of her looks in any particular way. She had a warm and pleasant face, certainly, with sometimes a faintly disturbing aura about her. Yet, seen in this light, her face gazing serenely at the lantern, he realized she was very beautiful.

"Well," he said, discomfited by this discovery of her, as much as by her words, "I'd better get going..."

He scrambled awkwardly to his feet, almost upsetting the tea tray in his haste.

He threw himself into his work, shoveling with furious energy on the ditch, trying to relieve some of the disturbing thoughts that ran through his mind. But the vision of Miyoshi gazing at the lantern came to his mind insistently, mixed with the images of her laughing, or sitting zazen, or sipping a cup of tea. All the images were delightful – and disturbing.

He had been working so intently, he had not noticed the threatening sky, nor paid attention to the rising wind. The force of the storm caught him by surprise. In minutes, he was knee-deep in mud, soaked through and through. He was halfway back to the house when he saw Miyoshi coming to get him with an umbrella.

"I don't think I'll need that," he laughed. "I'm all soaked already!"

"Come, I've got a bath ready for you," she shouted, for the wind carried her words away, and threatened to take the umbrella, too. Tadao tried to help her hold on to the umbrella, when a sudden gust tore it from her hands.

"Let it go! Let's get to the house," she said, and tried to run. But she slipped in the mud and Tadao was quickly at her side to help her up. Water streaming down their faces, he held her firmly round the waist and led her back to the house.

"Go ahead, the bath is ready," she panted, doubled over from the effort of fighting their way back to the house. But she was breathless, too, from the closeness of him, from the warm support of his arms. When they finally reached the house, she was shivering, not so much from the cold, but from his touch.

"How about you? You're all soaked and muddy, too. You can't just stand around shivering like that. Come on," he said, "We'll get cleaned up together."

She did not resist as he led her to the bathroom. Old Mr. Hasegawa had enjoyed the pleasures of the bath and accordingly had designed a spacious bathing area for washing up beside the big tub. The room was laid out as a bath in a hot spring resort. There were low stools, and buckets set around the washing area.

They sat on the low stools and Tadao scooped up a bucketful of water from the tub and poured it over her, then poured a bucketful on himself. It took most of the worst mud off. Miyoshi sat huddled as he poured still more water over her.

"We'd better take these wet clothes off," he said. She nodded and proceeded to pull off her wet clothes, dropping them beside his. They kept their back discreetly to each other as they undressed and as they soaped themselves clean. She kept her back to him, overcome with shyness, as he poured more water over her to rinse off the soap.

He handed her a small towel, then took one for himself. And, as if they were sharing a bath at a hot spring, or a public bath, they both stepped into the tub.

"Aah," she closed her eyes and gave herself up to the luxurious warmth. She had to close her eyes, too, because she was afraid to look at him. Afraid of all the disturbing, confusing feelings Tadao had aroused in her.

At first, he, too, was afraid to look at her. They had managed the whole washing process without seeing much more than each other's backs. But at last, he glanced covertly at her. Her closed eyes gave him license to look more boldly.

Sweat beaded her face, enhancing the soft glow of her skin. Her wet lashes lay long and dark against the paleness of her face. Her lips were moist and slightly parted, languid from the warm bath.

Tadao's breath seemed to stop, and in the timeless space between time and thought, he surrendered to the truth of his heart. Now he could not hold himself back. He moved to her. Softly and tenderly, he ran his fingers through the sweat of her brow. She opened her eyes slowly and gazed deeply into his. Her hands gripped her towel, but she felt no fear as she saw the look in his eyes. He moved his hand to cradle her chin and lifting it gently, he brought her face to his. He kissed her, the barest touch at first, and then more urgently.

Startled by the intensity of her own reaction, Miyoshi pulled away, gazing intently into his eyes, as if she could find the answer to her turmoil there. For a long moment, they stared at each other in bewilderment.

Then, overwhelmed and no longer able to control themselves, they melted into their passion.

CHAPTER SIX

Later, she could not remember how they had unfolded the futons, or that Tadao had called his home to explain that he was spending the night because of the storm. At one point, Miyoshi had the fleeting thought that Tadao was not exactly inexperienced in love, but any thoughts were fleeting, for she was caught up in a surging whirlwind of sensations.

She had explored his body, tentatively at first. His skin was so smooth and pale. He shivered as she traced lines around his nipples. He could feel his rising engorgement, and could not hold himself back. He took her breast in his mouth, suckling and teasing it until she moaned in pleasure. Hungrily, she gave herself up to him, responding to his urgency. She drank in the smell of him, the taste of him, the feel of his skin against hers, the sight of him in the dim light, so beautiful he seemed to her now. She had never been so caught up, so totally lost in her senses. Once she had given herself permission, there was no way to stop herself.

As for Tadao, his experience before had actually been few – some prostitutes and one young girl he had known in college. He had never known a full-blooded passion rising out of love. It was intoxicating. Miyoshi's passion had fired his own to heights he had never before experienced.

Frenzied, fervently, they spent the night making love, falling into an exhausted sleep, only to waken in a few hours, hands reaching for each other, wanting each other again.

They were hardly aware of the storm outside, so intense was the storm they created for themselves. The rain continued all night and was still coming down heavily when they woke the next morning. They were both ravenous for they had not eaten the night before.

"Stay," he said, "I'll fix something to eat."

"Ummm." She replied, drowsily, still holding his hand. He kissed her fingers lightly, got to his feet and went off to fix breakfast.

Half asleep, her body languid, soft and pliant as kneaded dough, Miyoshi listened to the rain falling steadily but softly now. She felt a warm gratitude to the rain for giving them this time, something magic, suspended out of ordinary time. She heard Tadao in the kitchen and saw him in her mind's eye, moving in his peculiarly graceful way, his hands so strong and masculine in contrast to the delicacy of his body. Softly, tears fell to her pillow as she thought, "How happy I am!" Her heart, in confinement for so long, rejoiced at being set free.

Thinking Miyoshi was asleep, Tadao tiptoed in, then seeing her tears, he enfolded her tenderly in his arms. He said nothing, but kissed the tears from her eyes and then cradled her head on his shoulder.

"It's because I'm so happy," she whispered.

"Yes, I know. It's the same for me," he said. They stayed still for a long moment, feeling the deep contentment of each other's quiet breathing.

"Breakfast is almost ready," he said, at last, "But the bath is just right now, if you'd like a bath before you eat."

"How thoughtful," her eyes said, and she thanked him with a smile, wrapped herself in a yukata and staggered to her feet, leaning against Tadao. She laughed weakly. "My legs feel like rubber," she giggled, as she went off to the bath.

The rain continued all that day, and for the next day as well. The ditch that Tadao had begun was washed away, but neither Miyoshi nor Tadao seemed to care. The garden was forgotten and the days were given to discovering each other. And to discovering themselves as well. Miyoshi's long dormant sexuality was matched by Tadao's vigorous young manhood. The were in turn playful, lusty, tender, bawdy, silly, serious, yet always attuned to each other's mood. Like children, they played at housekeeping, cooking and feeding each other, playing in the bath, scrubbing each other and sleeping at last in each other's arms. Even in their sleep, they held hands, as if they feared to lose contact in sleep.

On the third day, the sun came out. For once, Tadao looked at the sun reproachfully. There was no excuse to stay any longer. It would look bad if he did not go home that evening, but they still had that day. Reluctantly, he took his leave in the late afternoon. She watched at the garden gate as he went down the path. He kept stopping to wave to her every few feet, grinning and sometimes cavorting to amuse her.

When he was finally out of sight, Miyoshi went back to the house, still smiling at his endearing farewell. She went from room to room, tenderly picking up the things he had used and putting them away. The rooms were no longer empty, but filled with memories. Here, they had brought their breakfast tray…..Here, they sat zazen…..Here, he had taught her some Yoga….Here, they had slept….here,…and here…and here….they had made love. The house could scarcely contain her happiness and she had to go out on the veranda and open herself to her garden.

She gazed at Tadao's lantern. It had weathered the storm without mishap, though the garden itself was littered with debris from the storm. "He is truly and artist," she thought. And she wondered if she could help him out in some way, do something to help him develop his talents.

She imagined a life they could share, he making lanterns, or vases, or baskets – whatever he wished, and she writing her books. She saw a serene and idyllic life, the two of them sharing everything, doing so many things together. They could grow some of the herbs he talked about. They would finish the garden, of course, and it would be a wonderful place to sit and have tea. How happy they would be!

But as her picture of their life together unfolded, she also saw that all the relatives would be terribly shocked, would probably disapprove highly, at the very least. It would, in fact, create quite a scandal. She winced at the thought that Tadao might even be regarded as some kind of gigolo, interested in her for her money, and she would be seen as a sex-starved, perverted old woman finding delight in a young man. She had heard of bar owners and saloonkeepers in Tokyo – tough, hardened older women keeping young men. Even in a cosmopolitan and open-minded place as Tokyo, such women were looked on with contempt. What would a small village like theirs say about such a relationship..? She was fourteen….no, fifteen years older than Tadao! Would people look on them that way…?

It was a painful image. Quickly, she put it out of her mind. Yet it left a nagging doubt. How could she think of living with him, marrying him, even, a young man who still had his whole life ahead of him. He still had plenty of time to have a family of his own. She was beyond the childbearing age, even if she might have possibly conceived with a man other than Saburo. She would deny Tadao a family, and a respectable place in the community. How could she do this to him?

She had been brought up in a rigid Japanese society with strong rules about even the smallest things. A woman could not wear certain colors at a certain age, she could not go with arms bare, she should always be quiet and demure…….so many rules for every possible situation. How could she go against a lifetime of such conditioning and even consider such a thing as an affair with a much younger man......?

She was filled with remorse. She had no right to get involved with him, she scolded herself. She must break this off, for his sake. But the thought was unbearably painful. Her great happiness was still so new, so precious. She could not bear to have it snatched away so soon.

That night, her mind was in turmoil. She burrowed into her futon, where the scent of him still lingered. She held the pillow he had used, rocking herself as she held it, to console herself.

"Ah, my love," she whispered to the pillow, "I cannot let you go!" and tears spilled down the pillow.

It was nearly dawn when she fell asleep, and troubled dreams robbed her sleep of any rest.

CHAPTER SEVEN

Miyoshi managed to put her fears of the night before in some deep recess of her mind. The minute she saw Tadao the next morning, grinning his happy grin and sweeping her into his arms, she promptly put all her fears out of her mind and gave herself up to the joy of the moment.

They spent their days in the favorite pastimes of new lovers – being alone together, making the many delightful discoveries of each other, as if no other person in the world was as unique, as wonderful. The work of the garden went on in a casual fashion, as their mood dictated.

They had managed to divert the stream again so that part of it trickled into the garden and at one point, formed a shallow pool. If it was warm enough in the afternoon, it was there they would go to splash in the mud, reveling in the coolness of the water, the sensuous feel of mud on their naked bodies. Then they would have to go through the bathing ritual again, reliving the first moment of their love, discovering it all over again.

Miyoshi had done no writing since she started the garden. Once in a while, she felt a nudge from within, reminding her that she had promised her publisher a new book soon. But the sheer delight of the days quickly silenced that voice. She was having the kind of joy she had never known as a wife, the kind of delight she had never been able to have as a child. For Tadao was not only her lover, he was also her childhood playmate, and even sometimes, a wise roshi who would open her mind to new ways to look at her world.

As for Tadao, he settled into the relationship with a natural ease. For the first time in many months, he did not think of finding a goal for himself, or react to that inexorable pressure exerted on all Japanese to DO something. For a Japanese, to be idle was tantamount to the Western idea of sin. Tadao had been in disquietude within himself since he left the monastery, not knowing where he was going. His family did not suspect his troubled state of mind for he hid his feelings well. His joking, easy-going manner masked the confusion he felt, but the confusion had been with him constantly. Before, there was no one he could talk to about his feelings, even if he could have put it into words. At this point, however, when he was with Miyoshi, he did not feel the confusion so strongly.

Still, it was there and he knew he would have to deal with it some day. He wanted to know himself, to understand himself so that he would know what to do with his life. For it was obvious to him that at some point, he would have to settle into something. Japanese society does not tolerate an idler, and though Tadao had always been unconventional, he was not immune to the pressures and expectations exerted by the community, by his cultural heritage and by his educational conditioning.

This time with Miyoshi gave him a respite from his agonized self-questioning. He felt enormous relief in letting himself just enjoy the moment. With Miyoshi, he could defuse some of his turmoil by talking to her. For the first time, he had someone to whom he could reveal his wildest childhood dreams, or even his deepest fears. He knew instinctively that he could trust her, that she would not ridicule him, or make him feel stupid, as others had done in school, as the priests had done at the monastery. She accepted him, loved him, just as he was and this gave him a rare freedom to be himself, even if he could not still figure out who this "himself" was.

She, in turn, found in his openness, a rare intimacy she had never shared with anyone before. It made even the ordinary activities they shared a close, special bond. As a child, she had often scrubbed her older sister Kazuko's back but it always felt like a duty she owed to Kazuko by virtue of her status as older sister. With Saburo, she was always too nervous about his moods to be able to relax in the bath with him. But now, scrubbing each other's backs in the bath was an act of great tenderness that cleansed their souls as well as their bodies.

In this way, they let the leisurely days pass, with no thought for the consequences, or the future. As with the suspended time during the rainstorm, it was as if they lived in a world apart, in another dimension and time. And, indeed, in that quiet and isolated glen, they were in a world of their own.

However, Tadao always went home in the evening. It was an unspoken agreement between them, understood as necessary for the sake of propriety. They could no longer spend a whole night together and this was one thing that kept reminding them of the other world out there, the world that demanded a prescribed standard of behavior. They never discussed this world. To buttress themselves against this intrusion, they made their own day and night within the space of the day.

Tadao had to spend at least one day a week at home, for though Tadao and Miyoshi never discussed it, they both knew that their relationship needed to be kept secret. Miyoshi never told him of the dark thoughts she had had of the way their behavior would be seen by others. And though he had never said so, he had also considered the problems they would have in the village if people knew what had happened between them. They both sensed that for now, at least, their love could only exist in the glen. They did not want to think beyond that.

But as the days wore on and the weather became increasingly cooler, Miyoshi had to realize that one day her garden would be finished.

"Then there will be no reason for Tadao to come here," she thought, and the thought filled her with anguish. He had become so much a part of her life. He was, indeed, a part of her. She sometimes cried out against the fate that had brought Tadao into her life too late, then at other times she looked upon their love as a precious gift to be held for only a short time before it was returned. Yet, no matter how she looked at it, she had to face the fact that theirs was not a "suitable" match, and would someday have to end.

She wanted to stop time, to undo the work in the garden each night, so that there would always be something to be done, so the garden would never be finished. She had once read of an ancient king, whose garden was so magnificent, it had taken many, many years to finish it. Perhaps she could find some way to keep adding to her garden, she thought, but then she realized that Tadao could not make the garden his life's work.

Taiko came to visit one day and wanted to see how the garden was progressing. Luckily, she arrived when Miyoshi and Tadao were hard at work setting some stones into place.

"What a lot of work you've done!" exclaimed Taiko. "I see Tadao is doing a good job. I'm sure his mother will be very pleased to see how well he's working out."

"Yes, he's done a wonderful job," said Miyoshi, but she was loath to show Taiko around the garden and she held off Taiko's curiosity by guiding her away from the garden toward the house. The garden had come to be a place just for she and Tadao, not for anyone else. Taiko's presence would be an intrusion, a disturbance of the special harmony they had created. Each stone, each clump of moss whispered the deep bond between them and their creators.

"You're looking well, too," Taiko commented, as Miyoshi hurried them to the house to make tea. "I guess all this work in the garden is good for you, a good change from sitting at your desk all the time."

"Yes, I've always enjoyed working in a garden. I didn't realize how much I'd missed it living all those years in Tokyo." Deliberately, she served Taiko tea in the kitchen, where a Western style dining area had been set up. It was not the proper place to serve tea to a guest, but Taiko being a relative, it was acceptable.

"I'd show you the garden but it's not anywhere near being finished," she explained. "You were right. There is a lot of work to be done here."

"I see you've fixed up the front entry – that's a nice touch with all those river rocks along the path…oh, and you've had your kitchen window widened……" said Taiko, eyes narrowed pensively.

"Yes, Tadao did all that for me….he's been an enormous help…"

"Yes, indeed. It's really very nice, a lovely view of the mountains…"

Taiko had taken in every detail as she surveyed the house and garden. She was very pleased to see Miyoshi had taken her advice and finally was doing something with her house. Everything looked very nice; everything seemed to be going well, yet she had a disquieting feeling, something she could not put into words.

When she left, Taiko felt as if she had almost been rushed out of Miyoshi's house, in an unseemly haste. It was strange. Miyoshi was obviously happy with the garden and with Tadao's work, so her arrangement had worked out perfectly. So why did she feel so…..uneasy?

CHAPTER EIGHT

The weather turned cold and Miyoshi realized her glen would soon be snowbound. There would be little traffic to her house – only the weekly supplies, which came by sled during the winter. That meant there was also no reason for Tadao to be working in her garden. But Miyoshi could not bear the thought of being without Tadao.

"There is no garden work with the snows coming, but there is still work to be done around the house. I'd like to have some insulation put under the roof to make the attic into a usable room, for example. Do you think you would like to stay here and work for me…?" asked Miyoshi.

"Of course. I couldn't think of not being here with you. I'll explain to my parents that I'll be working for you. I'll say you are making a room for me in the attic…I don't really need to explain a lot to them. They're just as happy if I am working!" Tadao could not be sure this was so, but he preferred thinking that his parents did not mind. It made it easier for him, not having to make too many explanations to his family.

Miyoshi's house, built by old Mr. Hasegawa, had been built in the style of the old Japanese farmhouses of a hundred years ago. But being a man who liked his comfort, he had made modern improvements, like an electrically operated pump to provide water for the house, a generator to provide power for lights and appliances. He had even incorporated the idea of the Chinese bed loft, creating a heating system under the floor of the two rooms used for sleeping and general use. It made the house very livable even during the cold winters. It was convenient enough that Miyoshi could maintain it mostly by herself. She could get occasional help from the village for repairs or maintenance. It was a remarkable house, incorporating the beauty of the old-fashioned thatched house, with the comfort and convenience of a modern home. It was small, with only the two rooms, but by fixing the loft in the attic, it would create a good space for Miyoshi to make into a studio. There was certainly enough room for Tadao.

Just below the house, there was a good-sized barn-garage, which was no longer used, as Miyoshi did not own a horse, or car. Being on a lower hillock, it could not be seen from the house. Steps had been made for access, but were long unused. Tadao decided to make the building into a workshop for the work he was doing on the house. He also had an idea to do more work in stone. Making the garden lantern had gotten him interested in working with stone. He had a few tools given him by the stonemason friend and he was eager to try his hand at other projects.

Tadao was able to explain the situation to his parents, without mentioning his true relationship with Miyoshi. They did not think it too odd since she was a relative and was so much older than he was. It seemed like a good solution for taking care of both their needs. Tadao had explained all the work Miyoshi wanted done on her house to explain his reason for moving in during the snowbound season.

He packed a few of his personal things and moved into Miyoshi's house. They settled into a life together quite easily and naturally. Miyoshi went back to working on another book, though she did not spend as much time as she had before. Since Tadao had come into her life, writing did not seem so urgent. She had no particular book in mind, so it was easy to put it off, giving in to the pleasant distractions Tadao would find. He was constantly finding things to interest him, either in working with stone, or with baskets or paper lanterns. He had also brought along his books on gardening, special herbs and cures, and traditional folk arts and crafts. Miyoshi found it all very interesting as well, so that they had many talks about subjects in the books. This was real, this was life, and not the made-up kind she created in her romances. And it was so much more absorbing.

Tadao still woke very early, as was his habit at the monastery, and sat zazen while Miyoshi slept. He usually had breakfast for her by the time she woke up. The rest of the day was for his workshop, while she did the household chores. She prepared lunch and spent the afternoon at her work. They usually prepared dinner together a project that gave them both pleasure and playful delight.

Their lovemaking was relaxed and unpressured, with time to explore and make new discoveries. And often, they simply held each other through the night, content to be together, nestling like cubs in a warm den.

When the snow was very deep, Miyoshi helped Tadao shovel a path to allow the delivery sled to get through. They built a snow igloo one day, and sat inside with a candle and some hot tea. Tadao had not done such a thing since his childhood and since Miyoshi had never made a snow igloo, she shared his special delight. She had grown up outside of Tokyo, in a small farming community, which had been spared the worst of the bombings that leveled most of Tokyo. But with the deprivations of the time, she had no time or opportunity to explore the mountains or to play in the snow. Though she had lived in her glen for four years, she had not explored the area around her glen during the winter. Now she was learning so much from Tadao that he often seemed to be the older of the two. He was the one who introduced Miyoshi to snowshoes and cross-country skiing. It felt very awkward at first, but once she got into the rhythm of it, she found it easier and stimulating. It was a whole different world, to see her mountains like this in winter. Sometimes, they would flush out a snow rabbit, or some monkeys, and once, even a wild boar. The mountain was full of life, even in winter, and Miyoshi reveled in this discovery. Because of Tadao, Miyoshi was finding the joys she had missed all of her life. Tadao took great pleasure in introducing her to his childhood world and seeing the delight on her face.

The winter passed in this leisurely manner and Miyoshi did not mind if it never ended. She had never enjoyed her home or surroundings this way before. So when the snows began to melt, she felt some regret. Once the roads were passable again, Tadao would be going back to his home. He couldn't make excuses when the weather permitted access to the glen. Miyoshi would still see him during the day, but the luxury of spending days and nights together would be at an end. They never talked about their relationship, the propriety of it, the way it would be looked on by others, the future of it. By not talking about it, they could pretend they lived in this private world where everything they did was natural and right.

Yet somehow, deep inside, they knew that they still had to maintain outward appearances for the sake of his family. Only the thought that she would still see him almost every day made it bearable.

Looking back on it later, Miyoshi wondered if what her parents had always said was true – that mortals were not meant to have too much happiness. Perhaps it was doled out in carefully measured doses, as if the Gods did not believe humans could handle it. Age old Buddhist teachings had never taught happiness as a goal in life; had, in fact, taught that life was endless suffering. She had marveled at her good fortune in meeting Tadao. Had they been meant to meet? It almost seemed to have been arranged by fate. Surely it was no accident that they were so compatible. Sometimes she could not be sure if it were real or just another daydream from which she would soon awaken. After she had married Saburo, she realized that happiness was not to be found in marriage, or in a home without children. She had accepted that with Buddhist stoicism. Now she found it harder to accept. If she could be so happy with Tadao, why was it not acceptable? Most of the time, however, Miyoshi did not dwell on such unwelcome thoughts and simply lived each day without thinking about the future.

One morning, Miyoshi found a letter from Iwate, in her sister Kazuko's precise, neat hand. Even before she opened it, she felt a cold dread that made her hand tremble. She did not often receive letters from her sister. That, in itself, made her suspicious. She held the letter in her hand for a long time.

She had never been close to Kazuko. Their age difference of ten years as well as the difference in their personalities had always been too big a gap. Kazuko was a proud woman who had vowed long ago to make a good life for herself. She made elaborate five-year, ten-year and fifteen-year plans for her life, and had followed them diligently. Everything seemed to have worked out as planned. Kazuko always remembered the hardships of the war and postwar years with bitterness and this memory fueled her ambitions. Though she had married a minor official in the Iwate government, because of her constant pushing, he had risen to a rather prominent position there. They lived comfortably and enjoyed the prestige and respect of his position.

Kazuko had two children, a son and a daughter. This added to her feelings of superiority over her childless younger sister. As for Miyoshi, her husband had never gotten to more than a middle management level, so Kazuko felt herself considerably above Miyoshi in every way. As the older sister, she felt this was only natural.

Miyoshi's success as an author had come as a surprise to Kazuko. At first, it had annoyed her. How could that nothing of a girl, always mooning and daydreaming, achieve any kind of success? It suggested uncomfortably, that her well laid plans and years of struggle were open to question. Miyoshi had never worked as hard as she had to achieve her ambitions. If she accepted that success could come without so much effort, it would make a mockery of her formula, her efforts, and her sacrifices.

But eventually, she realized the value of a famous sister and she tried to share some of the reflected glory. She had begun a kind of desultory correspondence, which Miyoshi, in all honesty, could not say she enjoyed. Kazuo's letters always made her feel small and insignificant. The letters always reminded her of her lesser position so that it was a duty for her to respond, to remain the position of humble younger sister to assuage her sister's pride.

Kazuko had been a "kyoiku mama", one of those zealous, education-mad mothers and it was her top priority to get her son into all the "right" schools. As she had pushed her husband, so she pushed her son to excel in school. She had accomplished her goal and she was rewarded by his success, proud of his being so well placed now in an important government ministry. Miyoshi found this son a stiff and formal young man; always aloof, but condescendingly polite on those few occasions she had seen him. He was so cold and forbidding, it was difficult for Miyoshi to feel much of anything for him.

Her daughter, however, had been the exact opposite, a stain on the perfect family picture Kazuko had tried to create. Even as a child, Sachiko had rebelled against her mother's strict upbringing in every way she could. She had turned into a thin, nervous girl, high-strung and deliberately amoral. She had caused her mother enormous trouble and embarrassment during her wild years in High School. After High School, she refused to go on to college, saying she was bored with school. Sachiko's father found her a job, but she scoffed at the idea of work and instead, she enrolled in various courses as her whims dictated.

Kazuko had tried desperately to arrange a good marriage for her, as one way out of her dilemma. But Sachiko turned down any offers of an O-miai and dated whomever she pleased, usually a man she knew her parents would not like.

This was the situation Miyoshi's sister finally wrote about, reluctantly, to be sure. It was obviously a desperate, last resort. Kazuko wrote that Sachiko had run off to live with a man much older than her, a man reputed to be a member of the Yakuza. Sachiko had to be dragged home by her parents, who were keeping her momentarily confined. Kazuko asked Miyoshi if Sachiko could live with her for a while, at least until the scandal had cooled down enough for Sachiko to return home.

"You say your place is quiet and peaceful," wrote Kazuko. "It should be a good change for Sachiko. You're so isolated; she couldn't get into any trouble. And perhaps you would be a good influence on her."

Miyoshi sighed as she read the letter. She had not liked Sachiko any more than her brother. Though Sachiko had been a pretty child, her willful and spoiled ways had robbed her of any charm. Miyoshi had been glad that she lived in Tokyo and her sister in Iwate, which was far enough away that they did not have to see each other very often. Saburo had not liked Kazuko or her family and this, too, created much tension on the rare occasions that they got together.

Still, in some ways, Miyoshi also felt pity for Sachiko. She knew her sister's ambition; her strict and domineering ways were hard on the child. Kazuko had been equally domineering with Miyoshi during her childhood and had intimidated her into submission. Kazuko had always demanded such perfection from her children and it was easy for Miyoshi to see why Sachiko would rebel. It had been a number of years since Miyoshi had seen Sachiko. She must be about twenty-two or so by now, Miyoshi thought.

It was a problem for Miyoshi. She could not refuse to take Sachiko. Even if she was not close to her sister, she was too steeped in a sense of traditional family duty; she could not deny her own blood. She dreaded what this new development would do to the idyllic life she was living with Tadao. Though it was spring and the roads passable again, Tadao often stayed on at Miyoshi's, saying he was in the middle of a job to appease his parents. Having grown used to her life with Tadao, she hated the idea of giving it up and she felt a great resentment towards her sister for this untimely intrusion in her life. How could she and Tadao continue to work on the garden with Sachiko's presence to mar the harmony? How could they find moments to be alone, to make love, or just share quiet moments together?

Miyoshi agonized over the decision and at last she presented the problem to Tadao.

They were sitting on the veranda having tea made from loquat leaves. Tadao sat quietly, thinking over the situation. She left him in silence, knowing by now that this was his way, to think things over carefully before speaking his mind. This was how he had worked in the garden and he had always come up with good solutions. In the silence, she gazed into the pale peach brew in her teacup as if she might find some answer there.

"Of course you will have to take her in," he said, finally, for he had also had a strong sense of traditional duty. He looked thoughtful, but there was nothing more he could say. Quietly, his face resigned, he took her in his arms.

"We can't be together...we can't be alone...like this..." the reality of the situation struck him forcefully. Holding her, her did not want to think he could not freely hold her again. He stroked her cheek with infinite tenderness, soothed by the soft feel of her skin.

"I know...and I feel so terrible about it. I want to say 'no' but how can I? My sister has never asked me for any kind of help before. I know it must be very difficult for her to have to ask me for help. Yet...I...I wish I didn't have to do it..." Miyoshi's eyes filled with tears. Tadao, too, looked stricken.

"Anyway," she said at last, trying to bring some measure of comfort into the situation, "It won't be forever. Only until things calm down. Besides, Sachiko may not want to stay here, once she sees how it is here. She may hate it. It can't be very amusing for a young girl, isolated like this. We'll just have to wait and see."

They stayed in each other's arms the rest of the afternoon, cherishing their time together. Everything they did had a special piquancy heightened by the rushing hands of the clock. Miyoshi wanted to hold each memory to carry her through the difficult time ahead.

That night, Miyoshi called her sister and agreed to take Sachiko.

"It's got to be done right away. Sachiko is wild and angry and I don't know what she'll do," said Kazuko.

"All right. Send her to me as soon as you can, then. It will probably be lonely for her here, though. She may not find it very interesting or amusing," Miyoshi offered, hoping somehow that her sister would turn down Miyoshi's offer. But Kazuko had decided to send Sachiko and there was nothing more to be said.

"Well, I'll do my best for her," Miyoshi said with resignation.

As usual, Kazuko did not consider Miyoshi's feelings, assuming Miyoshi would do what she asked. She told Miyoshi she would send Sachiko the next day. Kazuko had never been to the house in the glen so Miyoshi had to give her detailed directions.

The next morning, when Tadao arrived as usual to make breakfast, Miyoshi told him the news.

"Today...so soon..." was all he could say.

"Yes, but not till this evening..."

Then we will make this a very special day for us. Hmmm....Now what can we do with this day...?"

"No work in the garden today. I declare this a holiday! Let's have a picnic lunch by the pool...."

Though she talked gaily, Miyoshi's heart was filled with a terrible heaviness. She felt as if a dark, evil presence hovered in the air. She tried to shake off the foreboding and make herself cheerful so as not to ruin their last day alone.

She went through the motions of making their picnic lunch with a smile on her face and listened to Tadao's amusing small talk. He, too, seemed intent on making himself as pleasant as possible to make this a special day.

They splashed and played in the pool and Tadao pretended to be a kappa, that mischievous turtle-like creature of Japanese mythology that dwelt in rivers and ponds, playing impish pranks on humans they encountered. Tadao said Miyoshi was a kappa because she loved cucumbers. It is well known that a kappa will do anything for a cucumber. Miyoshi laughed and said there were no female kappas, but Tadao one day brought her a small female kappa doll to prove his point. They made a big game of hiding the kappa doll in strange places for the other to find.

After lunch, they went back to the house and gently, tenderly, they made love. The realization that they would not be able to be alone for a while gave their lovemaking a special poignancy. It was sweet, it was violently ecstatic. And afterwards, they both cried softly as they held each other.

CHAPTER NINE

It was a sullen young woman who arrived at Miyoshi's door that evening. The long trip by train and then the bumpy ride by taxi up the mountain, had put her nerves ready to snap. She hated her mother for forcing her to leave, hated her Aunt though she didn't know her. She had to be a strange woman, anyway, living so far away from any human contact. What could she do in such a desolate place? She left it up to Miyoshi to take care of the taxi and to get most of the bags in the house.

She hardly spoke to Miyoshi, answering her questions with a brief "Yes", or "No", or a nod of her head. She maintained an expression of contemptuous boredom or resentment no matter how Miyoshi tried to coax her out of her mood. After a futile hour of trying to make conversation with Sachiko, Miyoshi gave up and showed Sachiko to her room, settled her for the night and prepared her own bed.

Miyoshi had trouble getting to sleep. She was thoroughly exasperated by Sachiko. To one of Miyoshi's generation, Sachiko seemed extraordinarily ill mannered and totally selfish. In the years Miyoshi grew up, no one had the luxury to indulge in personal idiosyncrasies. Miyoshi knew that many young Japanese today, brought up in a historically unusual affluence, were often spoiled by their parents. They were given things and permitted to do as they pleased. It gave the parents pleasure to be able to indulge their children in ways that they had never known. Though Miyoshi envied their freedom, she often felt irritated by their carefree, irresponsible ways. They had taken to imitating Western behavior, in every way. They looked with scorn on the old-fashioned ways of their parents and grandparents. Everything Western was good – everything Japanese was passé.

"We could never get away with such sulky, disrespectful behavior,"

Miyoshi muttered to herself. "These young people have never known any hardship or discipline, that's the trouble. They need hard work to straighten them out!"

Inwardly, Miyoshi vented her anger against her niece, then against Kazuko for raising such an ill-mannered girl. Kazuko, who took such pride in presenting a perfect picture of her family to the world, who always cared so much about appearances. What battles she must have had with Sachiko! This girl must have been very strong to resist Kazuko's stern upbringing.

Miyoshi made herself a pot of tea and took it out to the veranda where the calm moonlight would quiet her nerves. At last, her anger somewhat cooled, she had to admit to herself rather ruefully, that it was her own selfish desire to be alone with Tadao that caused so much resentment on her part. She sighed and resigned herself to the girl's presence with the same stoic attitude that had served her all during her marriage.

"I must endure it," she said, in the age-old admonition, and quelled her rebellious heart.

The next morning, Sachiko was in no way improved. She had now added to her sullenness a barely concealed contempt for her Aunt. Since she had grown up hearing only her mother's low opinion of Miyoshi, she simply treated her Aunt as her mother had always done. Besides that, Miyoshi was now in the same category as her mother – a meddling, old-fashioned jailer. She made no effort to help Miyoshi in any way, and showed no appreciation for anything Miyoshi tried to do for her.

Miyoshi sighed and put the best face to a bad situation, as her mother had always admonished her. She put on a cheerful face and served her niece a pleasant breakfast on the veranda. It was a wasted effort for Sachiko had no eye for scenic beauty. She picked idly at the food and paid scant attention when Tadao arrived for the day's work. He was merely a workman, not worth her interest.

Miyoshi was nervous as she introduced Sachiko to Tadao. She wondered if she would give herself away, or if Tadao would show her too much familiarity. But Tadao was properly polite and detached and soon excused himself to go to work. Sachiko noticed nothing, for she was totally wrapped up in her own misery. To be sent to this forsaken isolation was a severe punishment for a young girl who thrived on the incessant noise and loud blare of rock music, discos and bars. After breakfast, she turned on her tape recorder full blast to fill the unaccustomed silence.

Miyoshi winced as the sound shattered the peaceful stillness of her glen. She went out to the garden where Tadao was working, to get away from the noise, but it penetrated even to the far reaches of the garden. Tadao gave her a rueful grin and rolled his eyes up disdainfully in empathy with her distress. He understood perfectly how upset Miyoshi was and he did his best to distract her by getting her involved in the garden work.

They worked all morning in the garden, but the usual joy they found in their work was gone. Sachiko's music, her presence, had invaded the garden like a noisy plague of destructive insects. Now they had to curb all their natural feelings, to think before they spoke, to hold back from any intimacy. It felt intolerable to Miyoshi.

"Perhaps we should hold off work on the garden while Sachiko is here," Miyoshi suggested.

"She won't bother me at all," said Tadao. "I'm right in the middle of getting this pond and waterfall done. I don't want to stop just at this point." Tadao explained to Miyoshi that Sachiko's presence was no problem for him. He had worked very hard at the monastery to develop his power of concentration so he could tune out even Sachiko's loud, raucous rock music.

But for Miyoshi, it was not so easy to shut Sachiko off. She resented the loss of easy camaraderie and the relaxed intimacy she and Tadao had before. She missed the playful times, the tender loving, and the deep discussions. Now they could only discuss the more mundane things, or the work to be done. Chafing at the restrictions, Miyoshi wondered if she could keep up the pretense.

After several days of such unaccustomed inactivity, Sachiko became bored with her own company. She decided to see what her Aunt was up to. It would at least be a diversion to sneer at her Aunt's efforts to hide her annoyance. It sometimes amused Sachiko to see how desperately her Aunt tried to be cheerful and friendly.

"Such a dinosaur", thought Sachiko, putting Miyoshi in the category of all old people. They were all alike, and all boring.

Sachiko wandered out to the garden and as she approached the waterfall, she observed her Aunt and the gardener and her eyes widened, then narrowed in thought. She had noticed….something….perhaps in their pose…? Knowing nothing, and as thoughtless as she usually was of others, she still had an intuitive shrewdness about people. At an early age, even before she could speak, she had learned how to manipulate her parents and then others by studying their body language. Not that she had ever analyzed and intellectualized it as such. She had done what everyone does as part of their development, their natural growth, picking up messages from the world around her. She had simply been more adept, more cunning, in using her knowledge to get what she wanted. She had caught in a brief flash, a touch of intimacy between her Aunt and the young man. It was nothing she could have named, just a vague sense of something not quite right. It piqued her curiosity. Most interesting, she thought, and decided to study them more carefully.

For two people who had been as open and forthright in their love as Miyoshi and Tadao, it was impossible to hide their feelings completely. A look would linger too long, their bodies would naturally lean towards each other, their eyes would have a special sparkle.

Sachiko, who was now alerted and looking for signs of intimacy, soon found proof of her suspicions. She laughed to herself, incredulous at first, then contemptuously at Miyoshi,

"Why that pious old hypocrite!" She chuckled, "She's actually having an affair….with a man young enough to be her son! This is delicious!"

This was amusement indeed for Sachiko. It was an interesting game, a real challenge. Here she was being punished for having an affair with an inappropriate man, and she was sent off to, of all people, her Aunt – a woman who is having an inappropriate affair! This would be a diverting way to pass the time of her exile. She might pick up something to destroy this cozy little arrangement! Maybe she could even use it to her advantage to get her out of this dump.

In the next few days, Sachiko asked innocent seeming questions of her Aunt, to try to find out more about Tadao. Miyoshi did not suspect anything, thinking simply that her niece had finally decided to be more sociable. She was relieved at this new Sachiko and let down her guard. Sachiko had hit upon a plan and needed more information to carry it out. Cleverly drawn out, Miyoshi talked easily about Tadao. She never realized how warm or animated her face became when she talked of Tadao, but Sachiko noticed.

It disgusted her. She also observed Tadao closely, though she kept her distance from him.

"Tadao seems to be one of those sappy kind of guys, with a stupid soft heart," she said to herself. "The role of poor victim would probably appeal to him best," she decided.

She posed herself artfully against a curved willow tree trunk the next morning in exactly the place where Tadao was likely to pass by and see her. She had her head gracefully bent in sorrow. She could even force a few tears at the right moment.

She picked a time when Miyoshi was busy cleaning up after breakfast. She did not want her Aunt to interfere in this scene. She had timed it well, for Tadao made his appearance at the right moment. Out of the corner of her eyes, she saw him look at her, and then hesitate. She noticed with satisfaction that she had produced her desired effect, but she knew enough to stop before he took any action. She wanted him to be confused at this point.

A deep sigh escaped her and she made her way slowly back to the house, wiping at her tears.

During the next few days, Sachiko continued her mournful act, always where Tadao could "accidentally" see her. Once she noticed an agitated discussion going on between Tadao and her Aunt, with Tadao glancing covertly in her direction.

"Auntie looks pretty upset", Sachiko thought, and the thought gave her pleasure. "Tadao is just about ready to talk to me. I will have to plan our meeting carefully."

By listening to her Aunt's conversation with Tadao, Sachiko learned that Tadao would be going to the hilltop where the spring originated, and while there, he said he would pick some more leaves from the loquat tree for Miyoshi's tea. Miyoshi planned to stay in and do some writing that day.

Sachiko got to the loquat tree before Tadao and placed herself on a branch not too high up. When Tadao was within hearing distance, she snapped off a branch and fell to the ground with a scream of fear.

Tadao ran to her and fell on his knees beside her.

"Are you all right?" There was great concern on his face.

"Oh…" she moaned, "my ankle…oh, I must have twisted it…Ow!" She winced prettily.

"Here, here…let me see," said Tadao, gently moving her foot out from under her.

"Does this hurt…? Or this…?" he asked, as he slowly manipulated her foot.

"Oh, ow! Oh, no, it's all right….Oh, I'm sorry, oh, please…..don't fuss. It was so stupid of me…to fall like that…" feebly, Sachiko tried to get up.

"No, don't move. I'll help you. I'll carry you back to the house. We'll have your Aunt call a doctor. Maybe your foot's broken…don't try to walk on it."

"No, No! I don't want to bother my Aunt!" Sachiko cried, and burst into tears.

"There, there…it's all right….Please don't cry. We'll fix it right up…"

"It's not my foot….oh…I wish I had fallen from higher up ….and broken my neck! I wish I had killed myself!" Sachiko sobbed, now giving full rein to her tears. She thought of all the misery she had gone through with her parents and the tears came easily.

Tadao was taken aback by her outburst, but it was not unexpected. He knew she was upset about something by the way she had been behaving. Now he could no longer stand off in confused detachment. He moved to her and cradled her head on his shoulder.

"There, there," he soothed. "Don't say such things! You're so young…you've got your whole life still….there, there…" and he stroked her head.

"You don't know! You can't imagine what it's like," Sachiko wailed, but she gave Tadao no details. Gradually, she let his stroking calm her down.

"Let me help you back to the house," Tadao urged, but Sachiko frowned and shook her head.

"No...no...my foot's not broken, just a little sore. I don't want my Aunt to know. I don't want to cause her any trouble. My parents kicked me out of the house....I'm too much trouble, they said. If I make trouble, my Aunt will kick me out, too. Then where would I go? What could I do?" She sobbed anew.

Tadao felt a pang of pity. She was so small, so helpless, and so vulnerable. Somehow, he would try to help her. He would talk to Miyoshi. He would try to make her understand how Sachiko felt. He knew Miyoshi was kind; she would not kick Sachiko out. Sachiko had just misunderstood her Aunt's behavior, he thought, and he would help straighten things out between them.

He helped Sachiko to her feet and she tentatively took a step. She grimaced as if she were holding back great pain, but insisted she could walk. Slowly, they made their way back to the house, Tadao holding her arm, gazing at her with great concern.

This was how Miyoshi saw them approach the house. She was in the kitchen and with the large window Tadao had put in; she had a clear view of the path to the loquat tree. Sachiko had caught a glimpse of her Aunt at the window and smiled at her good luck. This was going to work out just as she had hoped.

Sachiko kept holding on to Tadao, though she did not really need his help. By then, she was walking quite normally, for in truth, there was nothing wrong with her foot. But she leaned on Tadao as if she still needed his support. Miyoshi saw only Tadao's arm around Sachiko, his eyes gazing deeply at her. Miyoshi caught her breath, a sharp pain clutched her so that she staggered and had to hold the edge of the sink to steady herself.

CHAPTER TEN

Miyoshi ran to the toilet. She had to hide herself, to be alone. She needed time to pull herself together. She could not let Tadao or Sachiko see her like this. The toilet was the only place where she could lock the door and keep Sachiko out. She could not bear to see Sachiko or Tadao at this moment. Pain, confusion, anger, bewilderment raged in a whirlwind around and inside her. She wanted to scream, to tear at her hair, to pound her fists on a wall until the pain of her body stilled the pain of her heart. Her face contorted into a demonic mask. She locked the toilet door, and clung to the towel rack, as spasms convulsed her body. Wails of anguish emerged as stifled sobs. Bile rose in her throat and she had to use all her years of stoic training to bring herself under control.

At last the effort to still her emotions drained her energies and she collapsed into a labored breathing. Again and again, her shocked mind tried to sort out her feelings. "Tadao..." she whispered, holding herself tightly, as if she could keep herself together by the power of her arms. She was terrified with the violence of her reaction. Even when she had suspected Saburo of having an affair, she had not felt such intense pain. By then, she had inured herself to his neglect. But Tadao – this was still so new. It was so …..unexpected. She had grown almost complacent in accepting Tadao's love for her. There had been no cooling of his ardor, no pulling away from her in any way. Her mind could not comprehend this sudden betrayal of her trust.

"Auntie!" Miyoshi heard Sachiko calling. For once, Sachiko's tone was polite and sweet.

"Auntie…? Where are you…?"

Miyoshi heard a whispered conversation between Tadao and Sachiko but she could not catch their words.

"I can't face them now," Miyoshi thought, and she tried to focus on a way out of her dilemma.

"Just a minute," Miyoshi called weakly. She heard Sachiko approach the door of the toilet, pressing against the door.

"Auntie…?"

"Yes…just a moment…My stomach's a bit upset…I'll be out soon…"

"Are you all right?"

"Yes, yes…of course. Just cramps. I think I might have a virus of some kind…Is there something you need…?"

"No…just that Tadao has to go…and…."

"That's all right. Tell him to take a few days off. I'd like to rest until this virus is gone."

"Is it that bad….?"

"It's all right! Nothing…just a virus. I'll be all right soon."

"Well…all right, then. I'll tell him you don't want him…for a few days…"

There was a satisfied smile at the corner of Sachiko's mouth, which she changed into a sad look as soon as she saw Tadao.

"My Aunt's not well – a virus, she says. She asked me to tell you not to come for a few days."

She sighed as she walked Tadao to the gate. "It will be so dreary here, with no one to talk to…..I guess that's why I was feeling so bad….before….."

"Now cheer up, Sachiko-san! Look – since I have some days off, why don't I take you to the village tomorrow? You can do some shopping and we can have lunch there. It will do you good to go out for a day."

"I don't know…..if I can…if Auntie lets me…."

"Of course she will. She will probably want to be alone and rest anyway."

"Wait here, then, while I ask her."

Sachiko hurried into the house but did not go to see Miyoshi. She checked to see if the toilet door was still closed. She went to her room and looked at herself in the mirror.

"What a good actress you are!" she told herself, well satisfied with her efforts. After lingering a suitable time, she rushed out of the house to where Tadao still waited.

"She said it's okay! She didn't like it, but she didn't feel like arguing, I guess. Look – it might be best if I met you down by that bamboo grove…I don't want Auntie to change her mind if she sees you at the door."

"Oh, I'm sure she won't…..Well, all right then. I'll be there tomorrow at ten – okay?"

"Fine! Oh, yes! Oh, how I look forward to it!"

Sachiko smiled her most fetching smile and was rewarded by a broad grin from Tadao. He waved and walked away. Sachiko noticed a definite bounce in his step and she was pleased.

Sachiko did not tell her Aunt about the next day's planned meeting with Tadao. They had a quiet dinner and retired early. Auntie really looks bad, Sachiko thought and for a moment, she wondered if her Aunt really was sick. She could not be absolutely sure since she had only caught a glimpse of her Aunt at the kitchen window when she and Tadao had come down the path, but she had a good hunch her Aunt was upset by the sight of she and Tadao together. After all, that had been the whole point of her drama at the loquat tree. Still, it was best to say nothing. In any case, her Aunt's illness fit right into her plans. Quickly, she put any concern for her Aunt out of her mind.

Miyoshi was still numbed by the emotional upheaval she had gone through and was very quiet, almost catatonic, through the preparation and eating of dinner. Even knowing Miyoshi was not well, Sachiko had not offered to help her get dinner. Miyoshi did not mind. She did not want Sachiko anywhere around her.

Miyoshi hardly ate any dinner. The food tasted like paste in her mouth. For once, it was Sachiko who tried to make conversation, and Miyoshi who sat numbly without a word.

The next morning, Sachiko found Miyoshi in bed at nine o'clock.

"Auntie, I'll go to the village and pick up some medicine and things to eat for you," Sachiko offered sweetly. "It probably isn't much of a village, but the walk will do me good. I've been cooped up here too long. Anything special you want me to pick up?"

"No, really. I don't need anything. The deliveryman will be here tomorrow anyway. I think I've got some medicine....please don't bother about me. Yes, do go to the village, though, and enjoy yourself. It will be good for you, I'm sure."

When Miyoshi was sure Sachiko was gone, she got weakly out of bed. She had to call Tadao and speak to him. She didn't know what she could say. She only knew she had to hear his voice. The night had been a torment for her, her mind going over everything that had happened the day before, imagining a hundred possible explanations for the scene she had witnessed. She wondered if Tadao had been interested in Sachiko long before and she had simply not noticed. She wondered how and when they had become so close. Those times she had been writing and Tadao worked in the garden alone…where had Sachiko been then? Had Sachiko been with Tadao then? She had been too wrapped up in her work to notice what Sachiko was doing.

She scolded herself for even wondering about Tadao and Sachiko. After all, they were both young people and she….she was being a foolish old woman.

"How could you even have thought of having a life with a man so much younger than yourself? Of course, it would only be natural for a young man like Tadao to be attracted to a pretty young woman like Sachiko."

She tried every argument she could think of to dissuade her from her attachment to Tadao. She told herself he was a young man with his life ahead of him, a life that included a wife and children. She had no right to keep him from such a life.

Yet all the arguments brought no answer, no relief from the pain in her heart. She yearned for Tadao with a hunger and longing that was palpable. She could not let him go now – not yet –not so soon! But Sachiko is the right age for him, she reasoned, and if he truly likes her, then I cannot stand in his way.

But….Sachiko! Miyoshi almost groaned her name. Sachiko – that willful, spoiled, self-centered….Miyoshi could hardly sputter out the words. Sachiko! Of all people! What could he see in her, Miyoshi wondered, outside of a surface beauty? Tadao was too fine, too sensitive, too intelligent, too good. Oh, how could he be so taken in by Sachiko! For she had, by now, assumed that Tadao had, indeed, been taken in, and seduced, for all she knew!

At that, her mind quieted at last. "What a foolish woman," she said to herself. "Making up all these stories before you even know what is happening! That's just like you – always making up stories! Talk to Tadao first. At least find out if it is true, if he is really interested in Sachiko."

She made herself a cup of tea to calm her nerves. She brewed it from the special herbs Tadao had picked for her, to soothe her nerves and help her sleep. Slowly, she sipped the tea and looked out on the garden. But the sight of it only brought her more pain. The place that had been such a joy to her was now a cruel reminder of what had been lost.

Angrily, she turned away from the garden and went to the phone. She called Tadao's number, but it was Misae who answered.

"Tadao...? Oh, yes. He's not here now. I believe he's gone shopping...yes, in the village. Do you want him to call you when he gets back? He said you weren't feeling well so he wasn't working for you for a few days. Are you all right? He said you had some kind of....virus..." Misae nattered on.

It was all Miyoshi could do to answer in a matter of fact way. She was torn inside with fresh doubts, new images – this time of Tadao and Sachiko in the village. Had they planned it this way? Did they want to be alone....away from her? Even if she talked to him, what good would it do? Would he admit to her that he was interested in Sachiko....?

Somehow, Miyoshi managed to end the conversation with Misae. She knew she must have sounded a bit strange, but she didn't care if Misae wondered about her. She knew Saburo's relatives thought she was strange anyway. It had never mattered to her before, nor did it now. She wanted only to be alone with her pain. For there was no one who could understand, no one she could talk to, to ease her burden.

Once more, Miyoshi turned to the garden. She gazed at it for a long time, letting the stabs of remembrance assault her until she had numbed herself. In time, the trickling sound of water, the quiet rustle of the reeds and a distant cooing bird song lulled her. She looked into the pond where a hypnotic image shimmered back at her.

"He's gone," she murmured and she fell into a deep, numbing nothingness of mind, which wrapped her into its comforting stillness.

CHAPTER ELEVEN

Tadao met Sachiko at the bamboo grove, far enough away from Miyoshi's house so there was no danger of being seen. Tadao felt a stab of guilt about sneaking around this way. He had nothing to hide from Miyoshi, but if Sachiko felt better this way, he was willing to humor her for now. It was the least he could do. His heart had gone out to her, seeing her suffering, as she seemed to be for the past few weeks. He had not dared approach her, not wanting to intrude when he knew so little about her. His natural delicacy had made him keep his distance.

    Yet he had noticed her sighing, mournful looks, the way she moped around the house, not paying attention to anyone or anything. He did not realize how much he had come to look for her, to see if she was all right.

    Sachiko had been well aware of the interest she had awakened in Tadao. This was her game, after all, and she knew each step, each move. She felt a mild contempt for the ease with which she had won her game. Not completely won over yet, she reminded herself, but it would not take much to have complete control over Tadao. She regretted that. It would take the fun out of the game. She had hoped he would be more of a challenge. Still, things were proceeding well.

Sachiko had put on a pink cotton dress that gave her a look of young innocence with its flounces, and a delicate embroidery around the collar. The fullness of the cut hid the natural gauntness of her spare frame. Her hair was curled and framed her face softly. A small pink bow completed the cute young girl effect, the look that was featured in all the magazines, guaranteed to appeal to Japanese males. She had on her most innocently cheerful face when she saw him at the bamboo grove. She almost skipped to meet him.

"Oh, what a wonderful day!" she called to him.

He smiled at her childlike enthusiasm. It made him happy to see her so cheerful for a change. She looked very appealing when she laughed and Tadao was soon caught up in her good humor.

Sachiko took his arm to walk more easily on the rutted dirt road. She did it quite naturally, as if he could protect her dainty feet from the dirt. She made the gesture very natural, as if they had been friends for years. She bounced along beside him, chattering about nothing and everything, agreeable small talk that required no thought on Tadao's part.

"Oh, what shall we do in the village?" she asked. "What is there to see….what kind of shops…? Restaurants…? I'm so starved for the sight of people! I don't know how Auntie can live in that terrible place, all alone like that! She's really strange, don't you think?"

"No, not really," Tadao said defensively. He had never thought Miyoshi strange. Quite the contrary. He had found her so much like himself that at times they seemed to think of the same thing at the same time. The synchronicity of their minds was a wonder to him.

"She's a writer so she needs to be alone to concentrate. It's easier to write when there's no disturbance around you, she says. And she likes the glen. It's really a beautiful place," Tadao said, caught up in the memory of the peaceful, happy times he had spent there.

"Well, I've seen much more beautiful places than that!" Sachiko pouted. "I could think of a thousand places that would be nicer than that old place! But everyone in the family says Aunt Miyoshi is strange so it's not surprising that she would live in such a place. I guess it's because she never had any children so she's all wrapped up in herself – that's what my mother says. I guess it's sad to be so old and all alone…" Sachiko looked covertly at Tadao, watching his face intently.

Tadao's brow furrowed and he fidgeted uncomfortably at the attack on Miyoshi. He hated to hear her being maligned in this way, yet he could not defend her too vigorously or it would seem out of place. He retreated into a pensive silence.

"Maybe I've gone too far," Sachiko thought, and quickly changed the topic and her mood. She realized that comments on Miyoshi would have to be more subtle. She needed Tadao on her side first.

"How do you know so much about gardening?" Sachiko asked, and smiled when she saw Tadao come out of his silence and back to his easy mood. He was too easy to handle.

Tadao modestly denied any great knowledge of gardening; just what he had learned at the monastery. Sachiko soon had him talking easily from then on. For the rest of the walk into the village, she maintained that light, easy conversation. Since Sachiko was good at small talk and Tadao was a good listener, they had a pleasant walk and arrived at the village in what seemed a very short time.

"Let's stop at a pharmacy first, so I can get some medicine for Auntie," Sachiko said. It would be good to impress Tadao with her kindness and thoughtfulness toward her Aunt, especially after the negative things she had said about her. It would also give her a chance to look at any new cosmetics they might have, or the latest gossip magazines; though Sachiko doubted they would have much in such a hick village.

Tadao led her to a small general store with a drug counter in the rear. There were only the basic necessities – aspirins, laxatives, antacids, antiseptics – and nothing much in the way of cosmetics. Sachiko sighed, with disappointment, yet it came out prettily as concern for the right medicine for her Aunt.

"My Aunt has s virus of some kind….it seems to affect her stomach…could you suggest something for that…?" Asked Sachiko, politely.

The Pharmacist, a pinched, ascetic looking man who suffered from ailments he had never learned to cure for himself, assumed a knowing expression to impress this visitor. He passed some powders to Sachiko.

"This should be very effective. There is a stomach virus going around and a lot of people are asking for this….. just follow the directions on the packet."

Her errand accomplished, Sachiko turned to Tadao.

"There! Now we can spend the rest of the time for us. Where shall we go….?"

"Well, you must be tired and thirsty after that long walk. How about some tea?"

"Ummm. Good idea!"

Tadao ushered Sachiko into a small teashop, a rustic looking low building with weathered signs outside. The interior was dark, with a faint, musty smell. This was actually a shop that sold tea in packets and gift cartons, not exactly the kind of teashop Sachiko had in mind. There was a small table, set aside for customers to sit and sample tea, but most of the space was taken up with cartons, tins and boxes of tea, as well as packets of rice crackers and sweets to accompany the tea. There were teacups, teapots and tea ceremony paraphernalia as well. It seemed as if every available nook or cranny was filled with dusty looking packets.

Sachiko looked on the shop with disdain. She wanted a glass and chrome affair, like a coffee shop, something very American looking, very trendy, with a jukebox and coffee served in smart demitasse cups. With some effort, she held in the contempt she felt and demurely accepted a cup of tea.

CHAPTER TWELVE

"She's still in bed," Sachiko whispered into the phone.

"Maybe I should come over, maybe there's something I can do to help…" Tadao suggested.

"No, no. Auntie said she didn't want to see anyone."

"But if she's really ill…."

"She doesn't need any help. There's nothing much to do anyway, it's only a virus. It'll go away in a few days. I guess at her age it takes a little longer to get well. But she told me not to make a fuss, just leave her alone. She hasn't got a fever or anything like that." Sachiko sighed. "It's so…. quiet….so boring around here. Isn't there anything to do anything…interesting…?"

"Well, we have a famous waterfall nearby. Would you like to go see that?" asked Tadao.

Sachiko's face was a moue of contempt, but she kept her voice cheerful.

"That sounds wonderful! Could you take me…. today…?"

"Well…are you sure….that is….if your Aunt is okay…"

"Of course! She told you to take a few days off anyway, didn't she?"

Tadao felt a pang of guilt, yet thinking it over, he realized that if he kept Sachiko away, it would probably help Miyoshi, make her feel better.

"Okay. I'll borrow my father's car and come and get you," he said.

"Oh, how kind you are, Tadao-san! It will make me so happy! I'll get ready right away….and oh, you can come to the house, instead of meeting me at the bamboo grove. I'll tell Auntie I'm going with you so it'll be okay."

Sachiko hurried to her Aunt's room to tell her about the outing. She could hardly wait to see the expression on Auntie's face when she heard the news.

"Obasan….? Excuse me…I just wanted to tell you I'm going out…Tadao-san has invited me to lunch. He says there's a famous waterfall around here and he's going to show me that. Isn't that nice? I've got to rush and get ready…"

Miyoshi heard the news, but revealed only a slight frown of pain, not quite the effect Sachiko had hoped for, but at least there had been some effect. Without waiting for a reply from Miyoshi, Sachiko quickly left the room.

Miyoshi sank deeper into her futon, trying to blot out the memory of Sachiko's face. She tried to put herself into a peaceful oblivion, forcing herself to breathe the way Tadao had taught her, to empty her mind. But images of Tadao with Sachiko intruded rudely into her consciousness.

An hour later, Tadao picked Sachiko up. Miyoshi heard the car drive up and Sachiko's gay voice calling out to Tadao in greeting. She winced, and then wrapped her silent cocoon around her again and this time she found oblivion in sleep.

Tadao soon left the dirt road and headed onto the main road leading up into the higher mountains. It was a still early spring at this altitude and the air was cold, but early blossoms on some of the trees and bushes brightened the mountainside with color.

"How Miyoshi would love this," Tadao thought, and promised himself he would take her as soon as she felt better.

Sachiko nattered on at first, but realized after a while that Tadao's mind was somewhere else. Angry at his lack of attention to her, she pouted, but kept quiet and considered her next move.

Tadao's attention was on the road and the beauty of the new green foliage. The air was clear this high in the mountains and Tadao gave himself up to the keen enjoyment of the beauty around him. He was so engrossed, it took a while for him to realize that Sachiko had stopped talking, and was sitting silently, hand to her forehead, a frown creasing her brow.

"What's wrong? Did you pick up the virus, too?" he asked.

"No."

"Do you feel sick…?" he asked more kindly, to make up for his previous inattention.

"No, I never get sick," she said curtly.

"What is it then?" he probed gently, not wanting to upset her.

Sachiko sighed deeply before she turned to face Tadao again.

"Well, it's about Auntie," Sachiko spoke hesitantly; as if she wasn't sure she could talk about this to Tadao. He gave her an encouraging look.

"Well…I think she wants me to go home. I know she doesn't like me."

"You mustn't think that. Your Aunt is a very kind person and if she seems sort of cold to you, it's just that she doesn't feel well, with that virus. I'm sure she wouldn't send you home."

"I think I should go home. I'm a lot of trouble to Auntie. I don't think she really wanted me to come here at all. She only took me in because my mother insisted. My mother can be pretty pushy. Mother's really tough....and she always gets her way....or else! And Auntie....well, she really is strange, you know, just like everybody says. You know, kind of like a hermit."

Tadao tried to find some way to answer but he could find nothing to say that would ease Sachiko's mind. Knowing how he and Miyoshi had felt about Sachiko coming to the glen, he couldn't deny that Miyoshi didn't want Sachiko around. He had felt the same way. Yet it seemed unnecessarily cruel to say so to Sachiko. He kept silent.

Sachiko sighed deeply again. "I know I'm a lot of trouble to my parents, too. That's what they're always telling me. If I just went home without some good explanation, they'd kill me! They'll think Auntie had kicked me out for doing something wrong and I'd really get it! They'll say I did something bad to Auntie...but honestly, Tadao-san, I didn't do anything!"

Tears formed and her voice choked as she dabbed her eyes daintily with her handkerchief. Just thinking about the injustice of being exiled to this horrible place was enough to make her cry.

"I know, I know," Tadao hastily assured her. "She's just out of sorts now, but give her some time. She'll be okay again soon, and then she'll be very nice to you again. I'm sure of it.

Tadao thought he needed some time alone with Miyoshi to explain Sachiko's situation. He was sure she would understand and treat Sachiko more kindly.

Sachiko looked unconvinced but she let the matter go for the moment. No use pressing Tadao too much. She sighed once more, however, before she let it go.

"Well, I hope you're right," she muttered.

"Sure I am. You'll see! Look, there's a little restaurant by the waterfall. They're famous for their fish, caught right there in the river. How about having some lunch there?"

"Ummmm…sounds good."

For the rest of the day, Sachiko was on her best behavior. She charmed Tadao with her youthful enthusiasm and admiration of the falls. She kept up a light conversation for a while, but as they were driving back, she gradually fell into an unnaturally gloomy silence. At first Tadao did not notice, but her silence called his attention to her.

"Is something bothering you…?" he asked.

"I….I wish we didn't have to go back…..It's been such a wonderful day…."

'Yes," he agreed, hesitating, not knowing what to say.

"Tadao-san…wait! Let's stop by the river – I just want to see it again, it was so beautiful…"

Not wanting to disturb her any more, Tadao parked in a secluded spot near the river. He led her to the water's edge and as they stood there, silently gazing on the rushing water, Sachiko started to shiver.

"Here…it's a bit chilly. You take my jacket," he offered as he draped it around her shoulders.

"You're so kind. I feel so comfortable, so safe when I'm with you. Here's let's sit here for awhile," she said, patting a spot next to her.

Tadao obliged, but sat a ways away from her.

"Not so far away, silly!" she laughed. "I won't bite you!"

He laughed with her, confused by her sudden changes of mood, but obediently moved closer to her.

"See!" she laughed again, pushing against him. "I'm not a wild beast that's going to eat you!" she said, pushing harder until he was flat on his back. She pretended to be a wild animal, attacking him, biting the arm that he put up in protest.

Before he could think about what was happening, she was on top of him, pinning him down, her mouth hungrily seeking his. Though he was bewildered by her unexpected behavior, he found himself responding to her kisses.

Sachiko knew how to arouse him. She had learned well from her Yakuza lover as well as other lovers she had had before him.

"I've wanted this so long…." She moaned. 'I know you've been watching me, too. I saw you…I know you've wanted it, too."

Whatever he might have replied, he could not deny his body's hungry response. Without thinking he responded to her steady rhythm. In only a few moments, he felt himself losing control. He exploded in a confused mixture of lust, anger and shame. Sachiko consumed him totally, leaving him drained.

They lay there for a long moment, until Sachiko's shivering brought him back to his senses.

"Sachiko…I'm ….I'm sorry….I…" he stammered.

She smiled languidly. He wasn't much of a lover, she thought, but it had been a long time since she had had any sex and it was better than nothing.

"Don't apologize. I'm not sorry. I wanted you. Come on, I'm getting cold. Let's go back."

Tadao drove back in silence, still not quite believing what had happened. He was not able to understand Sachiko at all, he realized. He had no experience with a woman like her – a woman, truly, and not an innocent girl as she looked. Not much experience at all, he thought ruefully.

When he returned her to the house in the glen, he dropped her at the door, but could not think of what to say.

"I'm sorry," was all he could mutter.

"It's okay. We didn't do anything wrong. We don't have to hide anything from Auntie, after all," Sachiko laughed as she got out

So Miyoshi heard the car drive up, heard Tadao's voice bidding Sachiko goodbye and her sweet response. She felt a stab of pain that made her double over and moan softly.

Sachiko came in, all smiles and cheerfully greeted her Aunt.

"Tadao-san took me to the falls….it was so beautiful! We had lunch there, some really delicious fish….we watched them catch it for us right there in the river and…" Sachiko's bubbling voice changed to one of concern as she observed her Aunt's face.

"Are you all right? You don't look well at all! Maybe I should call a doctor…?"

"No! No….I'm fine. Just a little weak from not eating much these past few days. I'll have some rice gruel later and I'll be fine. I think the worst of it is over," Miyoshi managed to say, though she wanted only for Sachiko to go away and leave her alone. She had enough images in her mind of the two of them together to torment her without needing to hear about it from Sachiko.

The next day, Sachiko saw that her Aunt was up and about and decided the timing was right for a talk. She approached Miyoshi as she sat on the veranda, looking quietly at the garden.

"Auntie…?"

"Yes…."

"I see you're much better today."

"Yes.."

"I've been thinking….well…maybe I'm too much trouble for you. I know you like to be alone. Do you think you could talk to my mother…convince her that I should go home…? I'm sure my parents are over their anger by now…" She glanced at Miyoshi's face, so still and lifeless, it seemed like a mask.

"I do appreciate your letting me stay here and all, but I'd like to get back to Iwate. I still have classes, you know….and…."

Miyoshi's relief at this request was tinged with bitterness. Yes, you can go now. You've done enough damage here, she thought. But her anger was stilled by her own sharp, critical inner voice. Quickly, she scolded herself, for such maudlin self-pity.

"What did you expect?" a voice jeered inside her head. "Did you think Tadao was for you?" Miyoshi glanced up to see Sachiko nervously tearing a hydrangea flower off the bush as she talked. She noticed the porcelain smoothness of Sachiko's perfectly manicured hands.

"Look at her hands...young, beautiful...look at yours – an old woman's hands...why wouldn't Tadao prefer her? It's only natural, after all, youth to youth. You're a damned old fool!"

Miyoshi finally looked directly at Sachiko, whose thin face made her eyes look larger, giving her an innocent, childlike look. Her nose was very elegant, her mouth a soft red plum. She's a lovely girl, though she is awfully thin, but that's not so bad these days, probably exactly right for the styles they're wearing now. Miyoshi could find no fault in Sachiko's appearance. But her character – she had large reservations about that. In spite of Sachiko's moments of sweetness and seeming kindness, Miyoshi strongly suspected Sachiko of using such devices only to manipulate things to her advantage. Kazuko had been a good teacher, but all Japanese women knew the uses of sweetness to attain their ends. Surface sweetness was second nature to them, a basic part of their cultural conditioning. Even the unnatural high-pitched voice used by women in social situations made them seem more childlike, evoking the male protective instinct. Women could see through this artifice, but men often did not. Still, it was not her business and if Tadao thought her sweet and liked her, she could not blame him.

"Sachiko," Miyoshi spoke slowly. She struggled to think each word through before she let it escape her lips.

"I am sure it is not much fun for you here. You want to be at home, and you should. I can understand ...how you must feel. I'll talk to your mother. I'm sure she will agree you've been away long enough."

Sachiko beamed. "Oh, thank you, Auntie. You've been so kind....you and Tadao-san...oh, by the way, I'm going to ask my father if he can find a good job for Tadao-san in Iwate. Tadao-san's so nice, such a fine person! And he's too smart to be stuck here working as a gardener! I'm sure my father can find him a really good position in Iwate."

Sachiko's words were like little pricks with a sharp knife to Miyoshi. She had to drop her head into her hands to hide her face, biting her lips to keep silent.

"Are you all right…?"

"Yes, just a little weak still. That….sounds fine…you just run along now, I'll talk to your mother."

"Great!" Sachiko jumped up. "I'll go tell Tadao-san. Oh, he'll be so pleased!"

For a long time, Miyoshi could not move from the veranda. Tears misted her vision so the garden was blurred; yet she kept staring at it, as if she would find some comfort there.

"No," she thought, "I can't rest here now. I need to get away." She thought of a hot spring she particularly liked. It had always been one of her favorite places, a place where she might find some peace and tranquility. She would go there as soon as she got rid of Sachiko.

CHAPTER THIRTEEN

The thought of Sachiko leaving gave Miyoshi the strength to pull herself together to call Kazuko. This time she would not let Kazuko have her way. Being the oldest sister, Kazuko always made it seem her god-given right, or certainly tradition-given right, to decide how things should be done. Miyoshi had always felt intimidated by Kazuko's bossy ways so for the most part, she had found it easier to go along with Kazuko's wishes rather than argue with her. Rebellion against Kazuko always meant the sentence of a black cloud of anger descending on the entire household, an anger that would sometimes last for weeks at a time. Though she thought she was no longer under Kazuko's thumb, still, rebellion made Miyoshi a bit squeamish. But she would have to be firm. She could not bear to have Sachiko around a moment longer.

    Like a samurai of long ago going into battle, Miyoshi carefully wrapped a soft flannel sash tightly around her middle. She put on a fresh kimono, tying the obi snugly. The tight bindings made her stand straighter, supported her so that she could feel strength slowly flowing through her.

When Sachiko left the house to go to the village – "to talk to Tadao-san," she said – Miyoshi called Kazuko.

"What's wrong?" Kazuko asked at once, on her guard. Anything having to do with Sachiko could be bad news.

"Nothing's wrong. Sachiko is fine. But I've had a bad virus of some kind and it's left me feeling very weak. I guess I've been working too hard on my garden and the writing, too, so I had no resistance. I've decided to go to a hot spring to recuperate for a while. I can't leave Sachiko here alone and she doesn't want to be tied down waiting on me."

"Oh. Sachiko's been all right, though? Behaved herself?"

"Yes, she's fine," Miyoshi brushed away her annoyance at Kazuko's total lack of interest or regard of her feelings. "But I don't want to leave her here all alone. This place takes a lot of upkeep. I'm used to it, but I think it would be scary for Sachiko to be here all alone. She's not used to such isolation. And she wants to get back to school, she says."

"You mean....you're sending her home..." Kazuko had to think this out.

"Yes. I think it would be best."

"Hmmm. Well, things have quieted down here. My husband put some pressure on that gangster Sachiko was involved with and he's gone. I guess it's all right for Sachiko to come home now. Maybe she has calmed down a bit, being way out there. All right then. Send her home."

"I'll be taking a train to Hakone, to the Anzai spa there, so I can take her that far. Then it won't be bad the rest of the way."

Kazuko was surprisingly agreeable, especially since Miyoshi made no mention of money. She cut the conversation short before Miyoshi would have a chance to say anything about the expenses of sending Sachiko home.

Miyoshi let out a sigh of relief when she put the phone down. "I don't know why I always let Kazuko get to me....so silly of me, after all these years. I must be really tired. Yes, I need to go to the hot spring and rest for awhile."

Miyoshi busied herself the rest of the day, packing her things, putting the house in order. She called to cancel her grocery orders and mail delivery for a week, possibly longer. She would decide that later. Now she wanted only to leave as soon as possible. There were too many reminders of Tadao here. Most of all, she needed to put all that behind her. She must accept the idea that Tadao could never be for her. What a romantic old fool she had been, living in a fantasy like one of her novels! But no matter how hard she chastised herself, the pain stayed like a hard lump in her chest.

Tadao brought Sachiko back that evening, bringing Miyoshi a nice assortment of sushi for her dinner. He wanted to see her, but was afraid to at the same time. He had missed seeing her those days when she had been so ill. He had talked to Sachiko that day. He thought he made it clear that he was not interested in Sachiko, that what had happened the day before was a crazy, impulsive thing and he didn't want to hurt Sachiko. She had taken it well, saying blithely that she quite understood. She was just feeling so low and wanted to be held and loved. She didn't hold it against him and it was all forgotten. All in all, he was relieved at her response and they had ended the day having a friendly early dinner. She had been in a good mood, especially now that Miyoshi had promised to get her back home. When he drove her back to Miyoshi's, he was a bit nervous about seeing Miyoshi again. He wished Sachiko were not there so that they could have their own private reunion, but it couldn't be helped.

"We already ate, Auntie, so this is all for you. You need to eat…you've gotten so thin!"

Tadao stepped into the room and was shocked to see how Miyoshi had changed. She was so pale, so gaunt. She had obviously been very ill and he felt terrible that he had been unable to help. He felt a pang of guilt for spending time with Sachiko when Miyoshi had been so ill. He yearned to hold her, cradle her head on his shoulder and keep her safe and warm. But in front of Sachiko, he could only murmur polite inquiries about Miyoshi's health. In frustration, he busied himself serving the sushi, making a pot of tea, anything to keep himself under control. Miyoshi seemed to be ignoring him completely.

Miyoshi told Sachiko about the conversation she had had with Kazuko and Sachiko jumped up, grabbing Tadao's hand.

"Oh, Tadao-san! Isn't that wonderful? Tomorrow....?" She turned back to Miyoshi. "I can really go tomorrow?"

"Yes, and I'll go as far as Hakone with you. I'm going to a hot spring for awhile. It will be good for my health..."

"You're going away...?" Tadao could only gape. "But....the garden..." He added lamely.

"It can stay as it is. Most of the work is done anyway..." Miyoshi could not look at Tadao's face. She was afraid of the tears that she would not be able to hold back if she saw his eyes.

"But..." Tadao looked at her intensely, trying to catch her eyes.

Sachiko jumped into the conversation, oblivious of the tension between them.

"But that's perfect!" she cried. "Tadao-san...I told my father about you. He said he would find a good position for you in Iwate. If Auntie doesn't need you any more, you can go up with me! Isn't that great? After all, you're not really a gardener...I mean....that's not your real work....."

"Yes. The garden is finished, Tadao-san. You can find a good job, I'm sure. This would be a good opportunity for you," said Miyoshi. The words sounded harsh from the control she had to exert to say them.

Tadao felt as if he had been slapped. What had happened to Miyoshi? So suddenly? He wanted to shake her, make her look at him, make her speak to him, to explain. But he could only stand helplessly in frustrated exasperation.

Finally, in a barely controlled rage, Tadao said, "Fine. I guess I'm fired then. I guess I'm available for work. All right, I'll go see Sachiko's father!" and he strode out of the room

Sachiko followed him to the gate.

"Oh, I'm so happy you're coming to Iwate! It'll make things so much easier....We can take that noon train," said Sachiko.

He turned to Sachiko as if noticing her for the first time. He had been so wrapped up in Miyoshi's strange behavior, he had not really paid attention to what Sachiko had been saying. He suddenly realized that she wanted him to go to Iwate, to work for her father. But he also realized that this meant he was to be considered as a prospective groom for Sachiko. And he had more or less agreed to go......He must have been crazy mad! That was hardly what he had in mind. He could not even consider such a possibility. He had agreed to meet Sachiko's father out of anger with Miyoshi. But he needed to put things straight to Sachiko, so she would not be hurt, would not misunderstand. He took a deep breath and forced himself to calm down and look at her. She seemed so small, so pathetic. Yet he sensed she had a very strong will, a strength that didn't need any help from him – or from anyone else. She would always land on her feet like a cat.

"No, you go ahead with your Aunt. I have things to do at home," he said.

"But Tadao-san...you said....I mean, I told my father....and he'll be waiting to meet you. He's got a lot of influence in Iwate. I know he can find just the right spot for you. And you'd love Iwate! It's much nicer than here, more things to do. The mountains are beautiful there, too, and there's great skiing in the winter..and..."

Tadao raised his hands to hold back the flood of words.

"Look, Sachiko-san," he hesitated, not wanting to hurt her feelings, "I'm sorry, but I can't go to Iwate with you. I only said I'd go because I was mad at your Aunt for firing me like that."

Sachiko seemed on the verge of tears. Tadao took her hand gently, "I need to stay here," he said, "to find out for myself what I want to do. I appreciate your thinking of me, talking to your father about a job for me. But I need time now to be alone, to work things out by myself."

"But….you said….I mean…I thought you liked me," she said plaintively.

"Yes, of course I like you. You're a nice girl, very charming. You should think of finding a nice man and settling down. I'm sure you won't have any trouble finding someone."

"Yes, but…"

"You'd better go in now. Don't worry. Everything will be all right."

Tadao drove slowly back to the village. He was calmer, but still confused and puzzled by Miyoshi's dismissal of him. What could have happened to make her change so? Was it just being so sick? Maybe it was the stress of having Sachiko around. Yes, that had been a terrible strain for both of them. Maybe that was it. Maybe if she had a good rest at the hot spring, she would feel like her old self again. And she could come back home, healthy and happy to have the place to themselves again. They could go back to their old life, they could finish the garden…he stopped. But she said the garden was finished. She had fired him! He could not believe it. He must talk to her, but not now. He would go to the hot spring, see her there. It would be a chance to heal their relationship as well as her health. With a hopeful heart, he continued on home.

"Tadao-san said he'd go on to Iwate in a few days," Sachiko announced as she entered the house. "So I'll meet him up there. Wow! I'd better hurry and get ready to go… what train are we catching?"

"There's a 10 am train. I'll have a taxi come to pick us up around 9 or 9:15."

"Fine...I'll go pack!"

Miyoshi felt all her carefully wrapped energy flowing out of her body. Wearily, she undid the obi and carefully folded her kimono. She slipped into a yukata and headed for the bath. A warm soak was what she needed, she thought. As she passed Sachiko's room, she heard the blast of Sachiko's music, the wild activity of her packing. Miyoshi prayed silently for strength enough to finally get Sachiko out of her life. Unbidden, the thought came to her. "...and to get Tadao out of your life, too."

CHAPTER FOURTEEN

Miyoshi slept from sheer exhaustion, but was up early to prepare for the trip. Sachiko had lolled in bed until the last minute and Miyoshi had to help her get the rest of her things together in time for the taxi. As she was putting the last bag in the hall, the phone rang. It was Tadao.

"Miyoshi-san, I have to see you. We need to talk."

"I can't....the taxi's here...I've got to go. Please, Tadao-san, please, just let me go."

"Not until we've at least talked." There was only silence in reply. "Okay, then. Which hot spring are you going to? You're going to Hakone, right? Is it that hot spring you told me about....that special place you liked so much...? What's that place called...?"

"I...um...ah...Anzai's...oh, Sachiko, take that blue bag. Look, Tadao-san, I've got to go. Please let it go....good bye."

Quickly, she hung up the phone and dashed out of the house.

Sachiko, still sleepy and churlish, spoke not a word to Miyoshi.

"Humph…not even time for a cup of coffee. What's the big rush, anyway…?" Sachiko thought, but she didn't want to talk to Miyoshi at the moment.

This suited Miyoshi perfectly. Her mind was still in turmoil, not helped a bit by Tadao's phone call. Now she just wanted to get away. She wished the taxi would go faster as it seemed to crawl on the dirt road. At the train station, she was in a feverish impatience, pacing up and down, fretting over the time Sachiko was taking to pick out some magazines. It seemed an eternity until the train pulled out, exactly on schedule.

Miyoshi sank into her seat and closed her eyes. It was not a fancy train like the Shinkansen, the Bullet Train. Only a small local line made the connection to Mishima, where she would get off for the hot spring and Sachiko could board the Shinkansen from there to go up to Iwate. It was a slow train, old and noisy and the seats were of slightly frayed velveteen rather hard and lumpy. It was making every stop, and seemed to stay in each station an extraordinarily long time. Sachiko had gotten some coffee at the station and she was in a slightly better humor, but she was still in no mood to talk. She opened her magazine. Time to get back to the real world, she thought. Now that she was on her way home, the drama she had created in the glen had lost its importance. More pressing was the questionable reception that awaited her at home. With trepidation, she wondered what her parents' mood would be. Actually, it was her mother she worried about. She could handle her father. She might have to convince her father to find Tadao a job to cover her story, if it ever came to that. But her father was easy to handle. It was a question of how malleable a mood her mother would be in. In a way, she was relieved that Tadao was not going to Iwate now. It would have been a little awkward. Oh, she could have handled it, but it's easier this way, she thought. It had been fun playing her little game, but it was only a distraction, hardly serious. She looked out of the corner of her eyes at her Aunt, sitting so quietly beside her, eyes closed. She looks like a haggard old woman, she thought, and chuckled to herself. I did Tadao a big favor, saving him from her clutches! He should be grateful to me! She smiled to herself. Yes, it had been amusing. Maybe she could still use this to her advantage in the future - if her mother got out of hand, she could tell her about Miyoshi's affair with her gardener! What a blow to her family pride! Pleased with herself, she turned her attention to the world of fashion and film star gossip.

The three car train racketed along at a leisurely pace, but finally, it arrived at Mishima. Miyoshi led Sachiko to the platform where the Shinkansen would be arriving and handed her the ticket. She said good-bye to Sachiko without a trace of warmth in her voice. She no longer cared and was too tired to pretend some feeling for this girl who had destroyed the beautiful paradise of her glen. Bitterly, she thought, blood relatives do not necessarily have a bond. And she had never felt close to Kazuko. Kazuko had always been that remote and godlike older sister who could do no wrong. She could only be the adoring and respectful little sister, but at times she hated her sister who never understood her, and only used Miyoshi to play out her role of the lordly and sometimes benevolent big sister. Perhaps the gap in their ages had been impossible to close.

Without bothering to see the train leave, as her normal politeness would have dictated, Miyoshi headed immediately for the line of taxis lined up by the station. The door of the first taxi in line opened quietly and automatically, beckoning her into it's immaculate, lace-lined interior. She gave the white-gloved driver the name of the hot spring and settled back into her seat. Realizing at last that Sachiko was really gone, she felt a great burden lifted. Yet the pain in her heart still felt as tight as ever.

She felt drained of all energy. Fortunately, the codified language of social intercourse, with appropriate phrases for every situation a person would encounter, made it possible for Miyoshi to conduct herself properly without even a thought. It was so ingrained into her, polite phrases fell automatically from her lips and no one would have guessed from her outward demeanor the emotional turmoil within. She was able to get herself settled into the inn, handling encounters with the manager, the maid, the attendants, with the proper courtesy, yet with minimum effort.

She followed the manager down a long hallway burnished to a soft shine by years of diligent swabbing and was shown into a suite of rooms facing a garden. She could hear the pleasant trickling sound of a waterfall nearby. The main room was light and airy, in the minimal elegance of the old Japanese style inn. The shoji screens were opened to the veranda, which gave onto a lovely view of a deep-forested mountain. The tatami mats were fragrant and springy under her feet. Fresh young plum blossoms were arranged tastefully in the alcove alongside a scroll picturing an old man standing bent over, beside a wind-blown pine tree, the wisdom and patience of long years brushed in a few telling lines.

Miyoshi sipped the tea, which the maid had brought on a tray with a sweet translucent bean jelly. She gazed at the scroll as she drank the tea, her attention caught by the expression of sad acceptance on the old man's face.

"There is pain in your eyes, too, grandfather. But you are so wise…maybe you can tell me how to ease this pain…?"

"Pain is from wanting. You wanted something that couldn't be. You wanted to hold on, but you must let go and find your way alone," the old man seemed to say to her. His kind face, with his sad, but knowing eyes, said, "I understand your pain. But it will pass in time."

"Will it…will it ever pass?" Miyoshi murmured. "Am I doing the right thing, to let go of Tadao?" she wondered. The right way, the right thing, as she had been raised to do. As she did in her childhood, as she did for Saburo, as she did all her life.

"I was a quiet little mouse who never made trouble, never spoke out, never protested. It's the best way, I guess.…

best for Tadao-san, maybe the best for me. It's what Japanese women have always had to do. But why is it always so much pain? Why is that always the best way?"

The old man in the scroll was silent now. Miyoshi sighed. Finally, she changed out of her traveling clothes and into the crisp, fresh yukata provided by the inn. She made her way down the hall again and around the bend, the door opened onto the outdoor bath. Miyoshi caught her breath at the beauty of the scene. This was what the hot spring was famous for, this natural mineral spring surrounded by mountains, a waterfall cascading down the rocks. The natural beauty had been artfully enhanced to produce a scene of great tranquility and harmony. A steamy mist rose from the hot, clear blue water, softening the line of rocks circling the variform lines of the outdoor bath. In a leveled space in front of the bath, there was a place to wash before going in to the water. Beside it was a rustic looking cabana where she could hang up her yukata. Taking off the yukata, she took a small white towel provided by the inn and a wooden basin to wash herself before going in to the bath. There were low stools in the washing area provided for the purpose, and after she had washed and rinsed off, she stepped gingerly into the steaming hot water. The rocks, which formed the sides of the bathing pool, had ledges in some places so bathers could sit comfortably, if they wished, covered up the neck in the soothing waters.

There were several ladies at the other end of the pool and an old gentleman was with them, but Miyoshi kept to herself, wanting to savor this time alone. It was a cool day, with a crisp bite to the wind, but it made the hot water of the pool bearable. Dainty, freshly green maples dipped their leaves toward the warm waters and soft moss lined the banks. High overhead, a falcon wheeled, his raucous cry faint, but enough to send some anxious birds twittering in the bushes. Insects in the tall grass beyond the rocks chirped, preparing their voices for the spring mating season.

Miyoshi closed her eyes, listening to the natural sounds around her, letting the sybaritic pleasure of the water envelop her. Soon she was deep in the water's voluptuous embrace. At some point, she opened her eyes briefly, as the other bathers made their way out of the pool. She nodded and smiled to them and they returned her greeting before they climbed out.

As this was not a holiday time, the inn did not have many guests. Realizing that she was alone, Miyoshi sank into the soothing water again. She closed her eyes, this time going more deeply into a trance-like dream. She shut out the world around her, all thoughts of the events of the past few weeks. As a child, she had always been able to escape her dreary surroundings by going into her dream world. She forced her mind to go back into the comfort of that well-remembered world. After a while, she was even able to brush away the disturbing images of Tadao induced by the sensual languor of the bath.

She didn't know how long she had been there, when she suddenly felt a touch on her arm. Startled, she opened her eyes wide and looked into Tadao's eyes.

"Tada..o..!" she gasped.

But he closed her mouth with his.

"How...did...you get here..?" She frantically pushed him aside, climbed out of the pool, grabbed a towel and tried to get away.

"Wait..! I drove here. I almost beat that old train!" he called, as she scrambled towards her clothes.

"You shouldn't have come…" she was almost in tears now. Hurriedly, she tied her yukata and tottered, still trying to fit her feet into her slippers as she stumbled towards her room. But he was right behind her, tying his yukata as he came. He was in the door before she could close it and he closed it behind him.

"Miyoshi-san…" his voice was a soft plea. "Please, at least talk to me. Tell me what happened. Why are you pushing me away? Have I done something…..said something…?"

Miyoshi sank onto a cushion and wrapped her arms around herself. But she could find no voice to answer him.

"You can't just tell me to go away like that. Unless… unless…you were only playing with me…before…" His face hardened at the thought. "But I know you weren't. And you did want to see me, or else you wouldn't have told me the name of this inn….."

She looked up at him at last. He was still wet from the bath, his long hair fell over his face. His skin glistened with moisture. How beautiful he looked…as if to mock her, to make it harder. With difficulty, she forced herself to speak.

"No. I was not playing with you."

"Then…why?"

"Tadao-san, I always knew we weren't …weren't … well…suitable for each other. I'm much too old for you. I knew this, yet I wouldn't let myself think of it. It was very selfish of me. It was my mistake."

"Age…yours, mine, it's meaningless. I don't think of you as any age. It's how we feel about each other that matters."

"I thought so, too," Miyoshi replied, "and when we're together, I feel that way, too. But when I saw you with Sachiko, I realized I was being very selfish. I had no right to keep you, to hold on to you. I felt I should release you, let you be free to choose someone more suitable for you…. more your own age. I knew Sachiko liked you…and you seemed to like her…."

"So that's it. You thought there was something between Sachiko and I…" Tadao felt a pang of guilt but he covered it with a smile, and then made a mock angry face at her. "You never asked me how I felt about her," he scolded. "You came to your own conclusions. I'm not interested in Sachiko. I just felt sorry for her. She just seemed so damned unhappy. If I wanted someone my own age, I would have married before now."

"Yes, that's it. You should be married. Should have a family of your own! It's the right thing to do. That's why I'm being …well…unfair to you, to keep you with me. Don't you see this…?"

"But I'm not thinking of marriage. I don't even know what I want to do with my life. Ever since I left the monastery, I've been feeling so…..lost. I've been so confused. Then I found I really enjoyed working on the garden and I love being with you. I knew the job couldn't go on forever… I can't go on drifting like this…"

"Exactly. That's why you should get married, get a steady job…"

"Why? Why is that so important…? Everyone is pressuring me about it. But is having a job so important? Even if it's just any kind of a job? Or even a job you hate? Is that all life is for? To work, to have children that you don't even have time for because you're too busy working? To spend your evening at bars because you have to drink to wash away the stress and dislike of your job….? To go home to find your children asleep, children who don't even know you..? Is that all life is about?"

Miyoshi was taken aback, yet she thought about Saburo and his bitterness at the emptiness he had felt. A salaryman's life never fulfilled him. He didn't even have a family to sacrifice his life for. In the end, it had all been meaningless.

"I've never thought about it that way," she said. "I've always done what was expected of me, I guess, what I was supposed to do. I guess we all do that….what we are supposed so do. I never thought I had any choices. But I did want to marry Saburo…and I wanted to have children…"

"Fine. If that's what you wanted," he answered, "but for me, I never wanted that. I always thought there was something more to life than some mindless job. I knew when I was only thirteen, that I would never marry. I don't want a family. Maybe I'm too selfish for that."

Gently, he took her in his arms. His fingers traced the line of her jaw, softening at last to his touch. He looked deeply into her eyes.

"If you always did what was expected of you, why did you write your books, then? That wasn't expected of you."

In spite of the weakness she felt coming over her at his touch, she was caught by his question. Up to now, she had only mouthed the usual responses, the standard replies. She was parroting the words she had heard all her life. But Tadao's questions could not be answered so easily.

"No, that wasn't expected, was it…? Nor even acceptable. My parents would never have allowed me to do anything like that…..If they had been living, they would have been horrified. It was the first time I did what I wanted to do, just for myself. And I couldn't even do it until after Saburo died….."

"And…are you glad you did?"

"Yes, of course! But it didn't matter, you see. Saburo was gone. No one cared what I did."

"So you were free…?"

"Yes…but you see, that's where you're different from me. People expect things of you. Your family wants you to marry and have a good job, isn't that so? That's what all families want for their children. And we have an obligation to our parents…"

"Why? Did I ask to be born?"

"Tadao-san!" Miyoshi was aghast. It sounded blasphemous. It questioned the very roots of Japanese society.

"No, listen. Why do we always have to do what is expected of us? Who decided that? My parents aren't living my life, so why should they decide what I do with it? I always felt there was something more. I was always searching. My parents seemed to understand and they've been good about letting me do what I wanted….until I came back from the monastery…"

There was a light tap on the door and the maid arrived with dinner. She looked at Tadao in surprise.

"Oh…they said one dinner…?" she murmured.

Tadao got quickly to his feet.

"Yes, I've arrived unexpectedly. But I've checked in…. I'd like dinner here, too, if that's possible…?" explained

Tadao. He gave the maid a charming smile. The maid looked a question at Miyoshi.

"Yes...it's all right. My...ah....cousin....just arrived. I'm sorry. I should have told you before, but I was in the bath...and...."

"It's no problem. I'll bring another dinner right away," the maid said pleasantly, and quickly left the room.

Tadao let out the laugh he had held in during the conversation with the maid. He was tickled at Miyoshi's discomfort, at the unconventional situation she was being forced to confront. He had completely recovered his good mood again. Being with Miyoshi, talking as they used to do, made him feel he'd come home. Quickly he moved over to Miyoshi's side again and held her, very tenderly at first, then gripping her tightly, so relieved to have her back again. He thought he never wanted to let her go.

Miyoshi was caught by surprise. Tadao had made her think, as he so often did, questioning her familiar guide-lines. It was disconcerting, yet in her heart, it had struck a responsive chord. She had always felt herself different from others, an outsider, only pretending to be like other people. She mouthed all the conventional phrases, but a part of her had always rebelled at it. If life had not been so hard when she was growing up, she might have questioned her parents more openly, but no one rebelled in those days. The whole country was under American occupation. No one questioned authority, certainly not a hungry wide-eyed child. She looked at Tadao in open surprise, searching his face for answers to questions he had raised. Cradling her face, he smiled at the puzzled expression on her face.

"How can you think of our ages! You are just a child, so innocent, so wonderfully naïve! You're not hard and grasping, like so many people these days. No, Miyoshi-san, I think you're too young for me!"

She pushed him aside quickly as she heard the maid sliding the door. Miyoshi flushed with embarrassment, but the maid was too polite, and too used to the vagaries of guests. She pretended not to notice anything amiss as she set the trays on the table. Smiling, she left the room.

"This looks wonderful!" Tadao exclaimed. Numerous dishes filled the tray, served on a tasteful variety of hand-made pottery that perfectly complemented the color and textures of the various dishes. There was friend shrimp curled on a slab of clay, garnished with bits of sea grasses. Wild mountain yams, local vegetables in delicate sweet-tart sauces, whole broiled fish, quail eggs, burdock roots, a clear soup with delicate bits of fish cake and watercress. Spring flowers were used as garnishes on some of the dishes. It looked very festive.

"Ah! This calls for something to drink! This is a celebration for us, after all!"

Miyoshi smiled, her fears and anxieties held at bay. She, too, wanted to unwind and celebrate, release all the tensions that Sachiko's visit had created.

"There's a refrigerator with liquor in it…over there," she pointed.

"Hey, this place is really well-stocked! There's everything here. What would you like? Whiskey, vodka, beer, wine, sake…"

"Hmm…I don't hold liquor well, but maybe I'll have a little sake."

Tadao poured her some sake and got a beer for himself.

"Kampai!" they clinked their glasses, eyes never leaving each other as they drank.

For the first time in many days, food tasted good to Miyoshi. Tadao, too, had a healthy appetite and they devoured the delicious food set before them.

Later, relaxed by the drink, the delicious food and another soak in the bath, Miyoshi settled languidly into a deep chaise on the veranda. Tadao leaned against the rail of the veranda, breathing deeply of the cool night air. Stars shimmered in the clear sky, dancing attendance on a queenly moon.

The maid came in quietly, cleared the dinner trays and prepared two futon mats side by side. Calling a pleasant "Good night", she left them alone again.

Tadao sat beside Miyoshi and taking her hand, he gently nuzzled her hair, drinking in the soft, clean scent. To her own surprise, tears gushed from her eyes.

"Maybe it's only a dream, but I never dreamt such happiness," she murmured in his ear.

He nibbled her ears playfully. "Is this a dream...?" And then her throat, "Or this...?", parted her yukata and brushed her nipples teasingly with his lips, "...or this....?"

Her body trembled at his touch, a moan of pleasure wafted from her lips. Without another word, he lifted her and carried her to the futon. She felt all the tension and anxiety wash away on a crest of passion.

CHAPTER FIFTEEN

The few days at the hot spring stretched into a week as Miyoshi and Tadao enjoyed relaxing baths, hiked the nearby mountains, and explored the coastline by car. There were not too many vacationers around now – the season began in late April and May, around the time of Golden Week, but some of the fine seafood restaurants were open and they ate their fill of the local delicacies.

No more mention was made of Sachiko. Both Miyoshi and Tadao had accepted the fact that the whole matter of Sachiko had been a misunderstanding that was best forgotten. For the most part, Miyoshi could forget the episode, but at times, especially at night, she would waken with a cold fear and reach out for Tadao. Always, he would waken, too, and hold her tenderly until she fell back asleep. He was all gentleness and kind attention, trying to banish all her fears.

Miyoshi was enjoying herself so much that it came to her with a stab of guilt that she owed her publisher an explanation for the long absence of any word from her. She had put off calling him since she had finished her last book, and though he had not called or pressured her, he had sent occasional notes asking how she was doing. She didn't want to reply in some vague way in a note and realized she should talk to him in person. Now that she was close to Tokyo, she suggested to Tadao that they include a stop in Tokyo as part of their impromptu vacation. Miyoshi could talk to Mr. Akai, her publisher, but she also wanted to show Tadao some of the Art Museums and Galleries in Tokyo. She knew his work was as good as some of the work in museums and she hoped to inspire him to continue to work in some area of art. She was particularly interested in a show of sculptures she had read about in the newspaper. It was a show of pieces by Isamu Noguchi, the Japanese-American sculptor whose work Miyoshi had seen before and admired so much. Tadao, with his experience with stone, would surely find it interesting, she thought.

She called and arranged to meet her publisher in two days time. She was a little nervous about the meeting, for though she knew Mr. Akai to be a very understanding Editor, she was not even sure herself how to explain her present state to him. She needed to ask for time to do some deeper study, or even, perhaps, to do nothing at all for a while. She felt she needed to make a break. Something nagged at her, a dissatisfaction with all she had done before. She needed time to think this through.

The situation with Sachiko had really shaken her, more than the surface agitation, but a deeper disturbance. She saw how much Tadao meant to her, how vulnerable she was. In spite of the blissful time at the hot spring, there was a constant conflict within; inner voices still whispered that they could never be together. She battled with her inner voices to be still. But the voices kept surfacing, hinting at some deeper issues she needed to face. It was all disconcerting in view of Tadao's attentiveness and ardor, but she knew that until she had resolved this conflict within, she could not concentrate on another of her light romances. She had been deeply changed by her love for Tadao and the idea of a frivolous young romance was too shallow to waste time writing. Yet how could she tell Mr. Akai that? She must tell him something plausible, not just some nebulous feeling of.... discontent?

They boarded the Shinkansen to Tokyo, deciding to leave the car in Mishima since it would be a nuisance having a car in Tokyo. Parking was impossible, and traffic too congested. Subways were the best way to get around in Tokyo anyway, faster and more convenient.

The Shinkansen was a far cry from the old local train she had taken to Mishima. The smooth, quiet efficiency was very soothing. Their seats were comfortable with wide windows to enjoy the spectacular views of Mount Fuji. A constant stream of vendors plied the aisles, their carts full of lunch boxes of all kinds. There were gift packages, too, of tea, sweets, dried squid or mushrooms, local pickles – everything to cater to the traveler.

Miyoshi felt languid, still, and years had dropped off her face and body. She felt a renewal of ebullience and energy. Tadao basked in her delight, finding joy in hers. Whatever worries he had about his future were put away in a corner of his mind. He lived now only for the moment, only to make Miyoshi happy.

They stopped at a quiet hotel in Tokyo, in an old section of town where there were still Japanese style inns. Miyoshi preferred the comfort, the food and ambience of the old inns. They had so much more character and charm than the impersonal western style hotels or modern pensions. There were many old wooden homes still left in this area, though these were starting to give away to the new style mansions, piling boxes of small apartments one on top of the other. This downtown area of Tokyo was a maze of crooked streets, winding every which way and it took someone who really knew the area not to get lost. But Miyoshi had lived in the area for many years and it was comfortably familiar to her.

Together, they explored the neighborhood and found quaint old shops – dyers, tatami makers, hand-made rice crackers and paper goods, old-fashioned sweets. There were all sorts of little nooks and crannies to discover in the many narrow alleyways. The neighborhood knew of the tiny eateries jammed into the alleys, run single-handedly by inspired chefs that served rare delicacies to a handful of regular customers.

    The next day, they went to the Museum of Art in Ueno Park first to see the Noguchi sculptures. It was a weekday so it was not too crowded and they could take their time looking at each piece. Miyoshi could feel Tadao's excitement and intense interest. Knowing his mood, she kept a respectful silence to let Tadao absorb it in his own way. He stopped before a huge stone set on a pillar of wood. It's surface had been so ingeniously worked, it embodied various different textures and even different colors in the stone, to create a stunning impact. Tadao had never seen anything like this, had no idea such things existed. Most of the work done by his stonemason friend in the village was traditional stone lanterns, monuments or garden sculptures. He felt an explosion in his mind, blowing away all his previous notions. Hungrily, he drank in the sensations. The impact was so great, he was not able to say a word. At one point, he turned to Miyoshi and knew at once that she knew exactly what he was feeling. A great love and gratitude swept over him. He found in her such a perfect empathy, something he had never found in anyone before. They needed no words, being part of a culture that intuits so well, that prizes this kind of silent understanding.

    They went to another Museum, but Tadao felt his mind too full to take in any more. Instead, they walked around Ueno Park and the lovely lotus pond of Shinobazu. They even stopped for a while at the zoo, enjoying the antics of the monkeys, the beauty of the tiger, the charm of the panda with her tiny cubs.

    Tadao was unusually subdued that evening, yet Miyoshi, also full of anxieties about the next day's meeting with Mr. Akai, felt comfortable in his silence. He sat zazen for a long time that evening and Miyoshi tried to sit for a while, too, to try to empty her mind. As they sank gratefully into the futon, however, Tadao's pent up energy gave urgent expression to his love-making. Even afterward, when he would normally have fallen into a deep sleep, he was restless and wide awake. Finally, he had a few drinks, and relaxed at last, he could talk to Miyoshi.

"That Noguchi sculpture…it was so amazing! So powerful! I can't put it into words, but I have never been so moved as I was today."

"Yes," Miyoshi smiled in agreement, "I had the same feeling. I saw some of his work in a book once, but the photographs don't begin to capture the feeling of actually seeing them…"

"I want to go back tomorrow. I have to see them again."

"That's a good idea. I'll be busy with Mr. Akai tomorrow anyway. And then I wanted to do some shopping. We can meet back here for dinner…?"

"Is that all right? You're worried about Mr. Akai, aren't you..? Will you be all right going alone..?"

"Yes, yes, of course! He's not an ogre! He's really very kind and understanding. I'm sure it will go well," she assured Tadao, with more confidence than she really felt.

He held her in his arms, her head nestled against his. She felt utterly content and secure in his love. She felt sure she would find the right words to speak to Mr. Akai. Tadao's strength seemed to give her greater confidence in herself.

The next day, she left for her meeting with Mr. Akai with a stronger heart fortified by the night before. She felt Tadao's support and understanding of her as a person, not just a lover, and it gave her great comfort.

Tadao returned eagerly to the Museum. He spent the entire day there, studying each piece almost microscopically. It was a great riddle that intrigued him. Where does this power come from – the power he could feel emanating from the stone itself? But it was not the stone; it was the life Noguchi had found in the soul of the stone. It excited him, leaving him restless and impatient to try his hand at shaping stone. The work he had done on Miyoshi's garden lantern was so crude, he thought, compared to work like this. He examined how each piece was shaped, worked, wondered how Noguchi had worked with such huge blocks of stone. Where did he find his stones? What tools did he use to get this effect? He was full of questions. In the Museum Book Shop, he found several books on Noguchi. He bought them all and spent the some time in the garden looking at the photographs of other works, equally stunning. He found himself going back again and again. It was not until they announced the Museum was closing that Tadao realized he had not even had lunch and now it was time to hurry back to meet Miyoshi for dinner.

He was eager now to see her, to talk to her about his day's discoveries. He could not hold his excitement in silence any more.

Miyoshi was ushered into Mr. Akai's office with great cordiality and respect. It was only her third visit there. She had preferred to conduct business matters with Mr. Akai by phone or mail rather than face the scrutiny and curiosity of the people at the office. Not that she needed to worry. The office was a bustle of activity with everyone too busy to pay much attention to her.

"How well you are looking, Kanazaki-san," Mr. Akai said, as he offered Miyoshi a chair in his cubicle. Though Mr. Akai was a Senior Editor, he had only a small space for his office. It was partitioned but not closed off from the rest of the cubicles in the large room so the hum and bustle of the others filtered into his office as well. Miyoshi had found this unnerving the first time she had met Mr. Akai at the office, but this time it did not bother her at all.

Mr. Akai was not a physically imposing man being not very much taller than Miyoshi. He was in his early fifties by now, she thought, but as energetic as he had been when she first met him. His round, genial face and expression sometimes belied his sharp business acumen. He talked in an easy, friendly manner to put her at her ease, yet she had the feeling he was scrutinizing her carefully, making mental notes as they chatted.

"Thank you," Miyoshi replied. "I've just had a very pleasant stay at a hot spring in Hakone so I feel especially refreshed."

"Ah, yes, Hakone. Wonderful place! How lucky you are! It's the perfect time of year to go, before the summer crowds get there and the air feels so good now….."

Pleasantries continued as an office lady brought in tea. It was a different office lady than the last time and Mr. Akai introduced her.

"This is Miss Endo. My last office lady got married several months ago. I keep losing all my good office ladies that way!" he laughed.

They continued the small talk, Miyoshi not quite knowing how to begin. Mr. Akai knew her well by now, and patiently waited until she was ready.

"Akai-san, you've been asking me about my next book," she ventured at last.

"Yes. Of course I am interested in your work. The last one is still selling quite well, but I'm sure your readers are waiting for your next one. I always wonder what your next book will be."

"Yes, well, you've been very patient and understanding and I do appreciate it. But I need to ask you for more patience now. I…..I feel I need some time, some free time, to do….nothing, perhaps. I want to try something different with my next book. Something with more depth, I think. I'm not sure yet, but I know I need to think this through."

Mr. Akai looked at Miyoshi thoughtfully. She looked wonderful, almost radiant. He knew she had had some experience that had changed her. Yet he knew her innate shyness and sense of privacy and would not intrude. Her books had been successful, but he had to agree they did not have much literary merit. Still, she had found a style that had appealed to a large, female readership. He would be very interested to see if she was making a major growth. Though it might disappoint her current readers who liked her romantic style, he was willing to take a chance on her, to see where she would go. He was sure he could, if necessary, bring her back to her present successful formula.

"Hmmm…" he replied, looking encouragingly at her. She blushed at his scrutiny.

"But you want to make changes…"

"Yes. I feel my books have been the kind of romantic dreaming of young girls."

"That's what your readers find so appealing."

"But, it seems somehow….shallow. There's more to romance than just idle dreams. There's so much……joy…and so much…pain…"

Mr. Akai was intrigued. Something had happened to Miyoshi. Something had affected her deeply. Strange… living alone in that deserted glen….what could have happened to her…?

"Ummm. Yes. I would be very interested to see what you are developing. Of course you will let me know when you have some outline ready…?"

"Yes, certainly. I would value your opinion. But… I'm not sure how long it will take," Miyoshi smiled ruefully. Now she knew Mr. Akai would be behind her, it gave her courage.

"Don't worry Kanazaki-san. I have full confidence in you. You're a hard worker, a good writer. I'm sure you will come up with something very interesting."

Miyoshi gave a small sigh of relief, not realizing she had almost been holding her breath.

"You are a treasure to us," said Mr. Akai, "one I would like to help and nurture in every way."

She bowed gratefully. "You are so kind and a great help to me. I hope to be worthy of your confidence.." The words were proper, but also heartfelt and Mr. Akai acknowledged them with a respectful bow.

Miyoshi left the office, footsteps light, a smile of relief danced on her lips.

"Why was I so afraid of Mr. Akai," she thought. "I am such a child, as Tadao says, always worrying what the 'grown-ups' will think! How silly for a woman of my age!"

"And why are you always so afraid?" the inner voice said. But Miyoshi was feeling too good and she pushed the voice deep inside.

She went to Mitsukoshi to do her shopping. She could shop for everything in the same place. She stopped at the restaurant in the department store to have a dish of noodles before tackling her shopping list.

With Saburo, she had always felt guilty about going shopping, always worrying about how much money she spent and if Saburo would approve. It still felt a little strange to indulge herself this way, but her happy mood encouraged her to splurge on things for Tadao and for herself as well.

She found a book on Modern Sculpture, which included works by Noguchi, which she bought for Tadao, and got some books for herself as well. Her arms full of parcels, the attendant at the door hailed a cab for her. Full of happy exhaustion and anticipation of seeing Tadao, she was not even perturbed by the noisy street or the slow crawl of the taxi, the scurrying crowds, and the frantic, frenzied pace of Tokyo. The Tokyo she had known during her days with Saburo had been intimidating. She had seldom gone shopping at the big department stores, staying mostly in their neighborhood. Now she found the blare of horns, the clanging and tootling blasts of music coming from the shops an exciting symphony. She wanted to sing, but she had enough proper restraint to keep her music to herself. Instead, she sang silently all the way to the inn.

CHAPTER SIXTEEN

That night, both Miyoshi and Tadao were in a fever of excitement. Tadao rambled on about sculpture, the Noguchi works, especially, as he shuffled delightedly through the book Miyoshi had bought for him.

"Here, see! This is what I mean…..look at the power in that piece of stone! It…it…exudes a kind of energy…" Tadao could find no words to express what he felt, and he looked sheepishly at Miyoshi and shrugged.

"Yes, yes, I see what you mean. I felt that in the stone lantern you made for me…that wasn't just the stone, but what you expressed with that stone. I always thought you were an artist, Tadao-san."

"I want to try…I want to do more….Miyoshi-san..How would it be…if I used the garage as a studio and worked with stone there…? I'd get tools…and for now, I'd work with stones I find on the mountain."

"It would be wonderful! Yes, of course, that's a perfect spot for you," replied Miyoshi.

"Would it…bother you…? I mean, I'd still work on the garden…and I'd do this in my spare time."

"I think it would work out very well....but, how about your family? Would they object to your doing this....?" she asked.

"I think they are pretty used to the idea of my working for you. They don't seem to mind even if I stay with you as I did all winter. They think it's okay, well, actually, they don't say anything. But since you're a relative, they don't say it's anything wrong."

And because I am so much older than you, they don't imagine there is anything wrong with the arrangement, Miyoshi thought to herself. But she did not want to say this to Tadao, or even think about it. It seemed as if everything would work out as she had imagined in her dreams.... Tadao, working on his various projects, she working on hers and sharing their lives.

Miyoshi told Tadao about her interview with Mr. Akai, and his kind concern. She had not even discussed this aspect of her writing with Tadao before, but he understood what she wanted to do.

"This is very good for you," he agreed, "and whatever direction your work takes you, I am sure it will be the right road for you. I'm really very impressed with your courage, your willingness to try different things. You give me the courage to go ahead with my ideas, too."

They agreed they wanted to get right back to the glen and get started on their new life. They were full of ideas on how to implement this change. How to fix the garage, would the noise of his work bother her, would there be enough space for him, how could they fix up the loft so it made a good place for her to work. Quickly, they packed their things and got the first train back to Mishima, where they picked up the car Tadao had been using. They took advantage of having the car to explore a few of the scenic areas on the way home, adding to the pleasure and happy memories of the trip.

By the time they reached the glen, they were in a fever to get started on the changes they had discussed.

Tadao explained to his parents about his new living arrangements, and though they looked very thoughtful, they did not oppose his plans. Tadao had always done whatever he wanted and they had never tried to control or direct him the way they did his brothers. It caused resentment from his brothers, but both of them had made successful lives for themselves and looked on Tadao as a freak and failure, helping to assuage their jealousy of his free and easy life. It did seem strange that Miyoshi would take such an interest in him, but since she had no children, it was probably a maternal interest she took in him, so his family thought. She had been alone a long time and it was probably good for her to have someone around. All in all, it seemed a fairly good situation. No one wanted to look into it too deeply.

For several months, Miyoshi and Tadao were caught up in their work to make the place accommodate their new plans. Never once did they talk about Sachiko. Everything that had happened with Sachiko was forgotten. Nothing had happened, after all, Miyoshi thought. It had all been like a nightmare and now that she had wakened from the dream, she was convinced that Tadao had had no feeling for Sachiko at all, that he had only been kind to her out of pity. She had jumped to conclusions about Sachiko and Tadao because of her own feelings of guilt about Tadao. She should have trusted him; she should have known that he really loved her. Now, Tadao was being so attentive, so loving, that she could not doubt his feeling for her.

Sachiko had returned home to a strained welcome. Her mother had looked her over suspiciously, but could find nothing to criticize. She kept her actions in the proper mode dictated by convention, even if she did them in a cool and detached way. With her former lover no longer around, she had nothing much to do. She had gone back to her classes and outwardly seemed more docile. In fact, her behavior was so above reproach that Kazuko had to admit that the stay with Miyoshi seemed to have done some good.

But Sachiko was not one to endure boredom for very long. She was not going to classes as she said to her mother, but hung around shopping malls, or at the movies or at Pachinko Parlors. Before long, she had struck up a relationship with a man who ran one of the parlors. The man was a bit older, handsome in a flashy way. He dressed sharply and had a seductive way with women. He was married and with a family, but that hardly deterred him from looking at any good-looking woman who might be interesting. He had a faintly disreputable reputation, which made him seem even more interesting to Sachiko. He paid flattering attention to her and squired her around to illicit clubs, which she found exciting. It was not long before they began frequenting Love Hotels, where he could use Sachiko as he pleased. Sachiko loved his attention, his vigorous lovemaking, and the gifts he showered on her.

After a few weeks, Kazuko began to suspect Sachiko was up to her old ways, but it was hard to find out exactly what was going on. Sachiko was being very discreet, yet Kazuko was no fool. Three months after she came back from Miyoshi's, Kazuko, going through the laundry, thought with a start, "Sachiko has not had her period for awhile." She noticed that Sachiko slept a lot, refusing to eat, and seemed pallid and nauseous quite frequently.

Sachiko tried to elude Kazuko whenever possible, but one day, Kazuko caught her in her room. She closed the door and confronted Sachiko directly. This was not a very Japanese way, but Kazuko would not waste time with Sachiko now. She needed some answers.

"What is going on..?" Kazuko demanded.

"Going on…? What do you mean…? Nothing. Nothing is going on."

"You know what I mean. You have not had your period for several months. Are you sick? Is there some problem?"

"No….no problem. I'm just tired. I'm trying to study very hard. I'm really trying to learn something….do something with my life…." Sachiko whimpered.

But Kazuko knew her too well to be fooled.

"You're pregnant, aren't you" she said harshly.

"What a crazy idea…." Sachiko started to protest, but seeing her mother's face, she realized she could not fool her. She had been concerned, herself, and was about to tell her lover that she thought she was pregnant, but had not yet worked up the nerve to do so. They had been careless quite often, when their lovemaking became so heated, they forgot about any cautions. She didn't think it would be a problem - that he would find some way to solve that, arrange an abortion, perhaps. But their affair had not been going on that long, only a few months, and she was not that sure of his affections. But how could she tell this to her mother? Sachiko thought frantically of a way out, a way to buy time.

"It was that man….that man at Aunt Miyoshi's…the one who worked on her garden. He…he seduced me! That was why I had to leave there! Mama, I didn't want to…I…" she blurted out, before she burst into tears.

Kazuko's face froze into a mask of shock and horror.

"Mama, you don't know what was going on there… they were having an affair - that gardener and Aunt Miyoshi…honest! I'm not lying!" Sachiko poured out a story of lust and degeneration that finally completely silenced her mother.

After a long silence, during which Sachiko kept up a piteous sobbing, Kazuko looked sternly at her daughter.

"I will investigate this. I will speak to Miyoshi and get to the bottom of this! You are to stay in your room. I will take you to Dr. Miyamoto tomorrow for an exam. You are not to say a word to anyone – do you understand? Not to anyone!"

Shaken to her core, Kazuko went slowly to her room and sank onto her bed. She needed to be very calm and sure before she called Miyoshi, but she would do so. Right now, she could not go to Miyoshi's to see her, as Sachiko had to be attended to first, but there would be a reckoning. Miyoshi had had her easy and heady life long enough! She was not going to get away with such scandalous behavior. It was incredible, that mousy little sister carrying on such a flagrant affair....so completely unsuitable! If....if it were true. Yet...if such a scandal ever came to light...it would reflect on her as well! To be the older sister of such a debauched woman...she would also be the object of shame! This was going to be difficult. She couldn't just confront Miyoshi... without knowing anything about this young man. Who was this man, this gardener? First she would have to find out. Didn't Sachiko mention a young man she wanted her father to meet – to find a position doe him in Iwate...? Could this be the same man? If so, why was he looking for a position in Iwate? What really was his relationship with Miyoshi? Kazuko did not totally believe Sachiko's story, as she knew her daughter often lied. But if she had been seduced by this man, and she was pregnant, the timing was about right.... and who else was she seeing since then...? Kazuko knew nothing about a man Sachiko was seeing at the present time. That Yakuza fellow had been gone since before Sachiko went to Miyoshi's....Questions whirled through her mind. She was still not sure she should tell her husband about this. No, she needed to find out what was going on – from Miyoshi. What a fool she had been to send Sachiko to Miyoshi! Miyoshi, with her pious reclusive ways, her lofty reputation – oh, it would be a pleasure to destroy that! Yet, the consequences would rebound to her. She had to handle this very carefully. Her eyes narrowed, Kazuko took out a pad and made notes. Ask Miyoshi: who is her gardener? What is her relationship to him? What was his relationship with Sachiko? Were they having an affair? Is that why you sent Sachiko back home? What does this....gardener...plan to do about the baby? No, maybe not that question – what would Miyoshi know. Besides, Miyoshi may not even know

Sachiko is pregnant. That is, IF Sachiko is pregnant. First things first. Get Sachiko checked out.

Determination had erased all other feelings from Kazuko's face. She was like a tigress defending her cubs, though that was hardly an apt metaphor for her situation. Her "cub" was a sly and treacherous creature that could not be trusted. But Kazuko was indeed a tigress, defending her own territory. She would find some way to resolve this, without causing any bad odor on her, or her family.

CHAPTER SEVENTEEN

Kazuko was up early the next morning, arranging for an appointment for Sachiko. She had not told her husband about this problem, knowing he would leave it all up to her in any case. So she waited until her husband had left for work before she made her calls. Sachiko was still confined to her room and Kazuko explained her absence at breakfast to her husband by saying Sachiko wasn't feeling well. She said she might take her to the Doctor as she hadn't had a checkup for a while, and she was looking a bit peaked. Her husband hardly listened to her explanations, being more immersed in the news on TV. Besides, house and children was his wife's domain and he took very little interest in those matters.

    She roused Sachiko, who protested at being wakened so early.

    "I'm sleepy," she mumbled. "I just feel so tired and sleepy….I need to sleep a little more…."

    "Never mind," Kazuko said harshly, pulling the futon cover off and bringing Sachiko roughly to a sitting position.

She was not going to brook any nonsense from Sachiko today.

"Get dressed. We have an appointment at nine o'clock with the doctor," Kazuko said brusquely. She picked out some clothes from Sachiko's closet and threw them on the bed.

"Go wash your face and brush your teeth. Do it! Do it now!"

Sachiko dragged herself to her feet and stumbled into the bathroom. Splashing water on her face did little to help her swollen eyes and puffy face. But her mother was giving her no opportunity to fix up her appearance. Sullenly, she brushed her teeth, then ran a brush over her hair.

"That's enough….you don't have to make up your face to try to impress anyone. The doctor will know what's up."

All this time, Kazuko would not leave the room. She was not going to let Sachiko out of her sight for a moment. She stood impatiently while Sachiko slowly pulled on her underwear, and then the dress Kazuko had laid out on the bed.

"Socks…socks…get some socks," Kazuko urged.

When they got downstairs, Sachiko asked if she could have something to drink. Kazuko grudgingly gave her a cup of coffee, but not much time to drink it. They bustled out of the house to find a taxi.

Sachiko huddled in the corner of the taxi until they reached Dr. Miyamoto's office. The receptionist was expecting them, after Kazuko's urgent phone call that morning, and ushered them directly into the doctor's office.

Dr. Miyamoto had known Sachiko since she was a child. He greeted her warmly and cheerfully, but she only looked down and refused to speak to him.

"She's not had her period for a few months….she feels nauseous, she says, and she is tired all the time," Kazuko explained. She hesitated to openly state her suspicions, but felt that was sufficient explanation for Dr. Miyamoto to go on with his examination. With that, Kazuko went out to wait in the reception room, while Dr. Miyamoto conducted his examination.

When Kazuko was called back in, Dr. Miyamoto asked her to take a seat.

"It seems Sachiko is pregnant, as you may have suspected. She claims she had been forced to have sex with a man in Shizuoka some three months ago. It's a bit hard to tell right now just how far along she is, but she could be about three months pregnant. She is healthy, otherwise, her vital organs are all sound, and she is quite able to have a normal pregnancy. However, if this was a case of…rape…. you may want to bring this to the attention of the Police."

"Never mind. It is not something you need to report," Kazuko said, hastily. "I know the man involved and we will take care of this matter on our own. In fact, he is a young man who is interested in Sachiko…and was perhaps, a bit too eager."

Dr. Miyamoto did not want to raise any questions, or cause any further complications.

"If that's the case, she can continue to come and see me, or I can refer her to an Obstetrician to continue her prenatal care and delivery."

"That will be fine. Thank you so much, Dr. Miyamoto. We are much obliged to you. I'm happy to know Sachiko is healthy. We will take care of everything else."

With much bowing and thanks, Kazuko and Sachiko left the doctor's office. But once they were back home, Kazuko turned furiously on Sachiko.

"Tell me exactly what happened," she demanded.

Sachiko sank onto her bed, wanting nothing more than to sleep and escape everything. She had to come up with something her mother would accept. She groaned, and slowly, hesitantly, came up with a story.

"Aunt Miyoshi and this gardener – he's her husband's cousin, or something like that…they….well, I noticed they were acting kind of funny. So I watched them…."

So far, so good. At least that's the truth.

"And then....one day...I saw them...kissing....I guess they didn't see me, but I was so shocked. They made it obvious that they didn't want me around. I guess I can see why. But I saw Tadao, that's the cousin, one day, and I said he and Aunt Miyoshi seemed to be pretty...well, close. So he got suspicious, and then he got angry and he grabbed me and asked me what I was talking about. So I said he and Aunt Miyoshi seem to be having an affair. Then he got really mad, and he threw me down on the ground... He said...are you jealous? Do you want some, too...? And I tried to scream, but he put his mouth on mine and then he started....started pulling down my panties....and then, and then....well, it really hurt...but he just kept on and on until....he just kind of exploded inside me. Then he was all....kind of shaking...and said I better not tell anyone about what happened...and I better not say anything about Aunt Miyoshi, or tell her anything....so I started crying, but he just kept telling me to shut up...and finally, he went away."

"Is this the same young man you talked to your father about...? The one you said wanted to find a job in Iwate...?" Kazuko was not quite sure she believed the whole story. If the man had done such a thing to her, why would she ask her father to find him a job in Iwate?

"No....no, that was before .....before he..." Sachiko protested.

"Why did you want him to come to Iwate?"

"Well, I thought he was a nice guy, at first. I mean, he seemed like such a nice person. And he wasn't doing much at Aunt Miyoshi's – just working on her garden. But he wasn't really a gardener. He was studying to be a priest, but he quit. He didn't know what to do with his life, so I was just....well, I was just trying to help him."

"Do you like him?"

"Well, I did, at first. I mean, he seemed so nice..."

"Then you would not object to marrying him....?"

"What!? Marry him? But...but...He...he raped me..."

"He seems to have wanted you enough..."

"But I...." Sachiko ran out of words. Marry Tadao? It was not what she had in mind at all! But she could see where her mother's mind was going. If Tadao was the father of the baby, he would marry her when he found out she was pregnant. That would save the honor of her family. They would find him a job in Iwate. That would shut everybody up. That was all her mother cared about – the reputation of the family.

In her misery, Sachiko could not think things out. She could not tell her mother that she had been having an affair with the Yakuza man. That would cause a huge scandal. And besides, that man had disappeared and he had a wife and several children already....he could hardly be made to marry her even though he was more likely the father of this child. No, marrying Tadao might be the way out. She didn't have to stay married to him, after all. It was easy enough to get a divorce. And that sappy Tadao would marry her, thinking he had made her pregnant...actually, it could solve a lot of problems. It could also...and a delicious thought came into mind...get back at Aunt Miyoshi! She could even have her lover on the side...after all; she didn't have to answer to Tadao.

"Well, since he is the father....I guess he would marry me," Sachiko said, in a small voice.

"I will talk to your father. He will find this man... Tadao...a job. You can stay with us until he is settled in his job and can support you and the baby. I'll call him immediately. Do you have his phone number...? And, for now, we will not talk to your Aunt Miyoshi about this. In fact, we will not talk to her at all. Whatever was going on between her and.....Tadao...will be over once he is in Iwate. We will arrange for a wedding, maybe not in Iwate... maybe....in Hawaii, perhaps. That's romantic. People will understand that."

Sachiko's mind was in a whirl. Her mother, with her incredible energy and determination, had worked the whole thing out! There would be no shame for Sachiko, or the family. And their baby…..well, not Tadao's baby, but he wouldn't know the difference. It's a pity she could not see Aunt Miyoshi's face when she found out she and Tadao had gotten married!

CHAPTER EIGHTEEN

Miyoshi and Tadao settled easily into their new life in the glen. They were both caught up in making the changes to the house and the space that would be Tadao's new workshop, and moving Miyoshi into the loft space for her work. They fell into the project with great enthusiasm and gusto.

It was hard work at times, and Tadao sometimes felt he was asking too much of Miyoshi, but she insisted she was up to it. In fact, she had never remembered enjoying anything so much. It was a kind of game she played as a child, making little houses out of scraps of wood for her paper dolls to inhabit. But this was much more fun, and doing it with Tadao made it light work.

They would soak gratefully into the bath each night, muscles aching, but feeling happy about the day's progress. Miyoshi loved to scrub Tadao's lean body, to feel the smoothness of his skin and the toughness of the muscles just below. He was just this contrast of soft and tough in his lovemaking as well. Some nights, he wanted only to hold her from behind, his arms wrapped around her, cupping her breasts, his legs curling her into a fetal position. It was tender and gentle, his soft breathing on her neck lulling her to sleep.

Sometimes their lovemaking was full of laughter and play. They would tease each other until play turned into passion. Miyoshi found his changes of mood an exciting preview of what would come later that night. When he was struggling with some problem, he might turn savage and attack her with a primitive lust that brought her to her knees.

For Tadao, he found she matched him in ardor and appetite, so that he could indulge in his wildest fantasies. Both were discovering all the delights of their bodies for the first time.

But all the pleasure he found in lovemaking was matched by the pleasure of her company in all the small things they did together. Cooking a meal was an adventure. Working on the house or garden, they both fell into the work with complete concentration of effort so that the hardest work became challenging and satisfying.

Miyoshi had put Sachiko completely out of her mind. Tadao never spoke of her, either, as if both of them wanted to erase that part of their lives. Miyoshi felt so sure of Tadao's love for her every day, in everything he did.

He showed his love in so many ways. Some evenings, when they had been working very hard on the house or garden, Tadao would warm up a cake of konnyaku, wrap it up in a towel and apply it to Miyoshi's shoulders or neck. Then he would gently work his fingers around her sore muscles until she felt soft and supple again.

Miyoshi had the small, impish looking kappa doll, which Tadao had given her. She laughingly called the kappa, Tadao, claiming he was really a kappa. Tadao insisted she was the kappa, that she was the mischievous one who had him under her spell.

"But kappas are males," she protested, "and see, he even looks like you!"

"Kappas are male AND female! And female ones are the most mischievous," he said, with utter seriousness. They never tired of this private joke about kappas.

She took to hiding the doll in odd places so he could find it – among his underwear, or in his tea cup. It became a game, and he would, in turn, hide the creature somewhere to surprise her.

Several months passed in this fashion, and they grew familiar with the rhythm of their life. Once Miyoshi's loft space was ready, she had settled her desk in and started writing again. But her writing did not flow, as it had done before. She tried outlining and organizing a skeleton of a story, hoping to flesh it out as she went on, but that wasn't working either. It almost seemed as if her writing had been dependent on the emptiness of her personal life. Now that Tadao filled her life so completely, she had no need to write about anything. Her creative energies were now going into the garden, or their meals, or little touches she made in her home. After a number of false starts and blocked thoughts, she talked to Tadao about her frustration with her work.

"You've been working so hard, for so long, maybe it's time you just did nothing. Maybe you need to take a vacation from writing. We've been doing so much with the garden, and you enjoy it so much, maybe that is enough for you for now," he suggested.

"You're probably right….and I do want to do some other kind of writing – not any more of those silly romances! Tadao-san, the reality of love is so different from the girlish dreams I once had! Maybe I don't want to write about love at all…it's better to love than to write about love, after all," she laughed.

"It's definitely better," he agreed, lifting her into his arms and carrying her to their bed.

Having all their time at their disposal, to do as they wished, they learned to divide their labors so there was always time for play. There was no one to tell them what to do; yet they fell into a natural pattern. They had created a perfect little world for themselves and had no thought that anything could happen to disturb it.

One day, Tadao had been up early, and was down at the riverbed, looking for stones for his work. It was heavy work and he wanted to do it before the sun got too hot. He could hear the early buzzing of the cicadas, warning him it would be another hot and sultry day. He was intent on his search for a good rock and at first, he did not hear Miyoshi calling him.

"Tadao-san!" her voice finally came to him from the hillock above the river. He looked up and saw her waving and signaling for him to come up. Since he had found no rock that exactly suited him, he went up the hill immediately to see what Miyoshi wanted. Normally, she did not bother him, so it must be something important, he thought.

"It's your mother…on the phone. She says she needs to talk to you…that it's urgent," explained Miyoshi, when Tadao was within hearing distance. "I told her I'd find you and have you call her right back."

"What's happening? Did she say what she wanted…. what was so urgent?" he asked.

"No. Nothing. Just that you were to call her right away," said Miyoshi. A puzzled frown on her face, she took Tadao's arm and went back to the house. It was unusual for Tadao's family to call him. They had accepted that he was working with Miyoshi and did not want to pry into the matter any further.

Tadao called his mother at once, a look of worry on his face.

"Mother…what is happening…? Are you all right? Is father all right..? Is…"

"Tadao ….listen. A woman named Sachiko says she needs to speak to you at once. She says it is very urgent, but she won't explain why. She just kept saying she must talk to you, immediately. Here is her number…0465-36-5521, did you get that? She was very, very insistent. I don't know what it is, but she kept saying it is very urgent," Misae said. "I don't even know anyone named Sachiko…in Iwate…? Who is she…?"

Tadao froze. A call from Sachiko would not be good news, no matter what. It might be she had found a job for him, after all. She liked to dramatize things – maybe she wanted it to sound urgent. And she didn't like her Aunt, so she would not call at the house. Somehow, she had managed to locate his parents...

"All right, mother. I'll call her. It may be about a job. She said her father was going to try to find me a job in Iwate," Tadao explained.

"Well, why is it so urgent...?" asked Misae.

"Sachiko is...well, she's a person who likes to make herself important..." Tadao said, not wanting to mention that Sachiko was Miyoshi's niece. His mother would think it very strange that Sachiko would not call her own Aunt, rather than try to reach Tadao at his home. He did not want his family to know anything about Sachiko, in any case. He took down the phone number and told his mother not to worry – it was probably nothing at all. Besides, he was busy working at Miyoshi's right now and was not interested in a job in Iwate.

Miyoshi heard his part of the conversation and immediately, her heart sank. She knew that Sachiko could be up to no good – but what could she need to talk to Tadao about, so urgently? A shiver went through her in spite of the heat of the day, as if a cold hand had pressed on her breast.

Tadao turned to Miyoshi when he put down the phone, and saw the look of anxiety on her face.

"It's Sachiko...wants to talk to me. Says it's urgent. I'll bet it's that job she said she was going to ask her father to find for me," he said, making his voice as nonchalant as possible to assuage her fears. But he was far from feeling so confident. However, there was nothing for it but to call.

When he rang the number, a woman answered – not Sachiko.

"Moshi, moshi," Tadao began, and introduced himself, asking to speak to Sachiko.

"In just a moment, I will let you speak to her. But first, I have something to say to you. I am Sachiko's mother. She has told me what happened to her when she was staying at my sister's home. To say that I am disgusted is being very polite. You took advantage of my daughter – and now she is pregnant. I don't know what you told her, but you have an obligation to marry her. I will not allow my daughter's name to be dragged in the mud because of your lust. You will prepare to meet Sachiko in Tokyo, and then the two of you will fly to Hawaii to get married. I will not say anything more. But if you do not do this at once, I will have to talk to my sister about what happened between you and my daughter. If you do not want me to say anything to her, you will do as I say. Now, I'll let you talk to Sachiko."

During this entire pronouncement, Tadao stood frozen in shocked silence. He could hardly take in what she was saying; yet slowly it penetrated. Sachiko was pregnant. And he had indeed had sex with her that one time...and it was just about three months ago. He could not deny that, or deny that he fathered her child. But it was all too much to take in at once. When Sachiko came on the line, he could barely speak.

"Sachiko...I...I don't know what to say," he stammered. "Is it .....is it true? I mean..."

"Of course it's true!" Sachiko wailed. "I wouldn't make up a thing like that! My mother took me to the doctor and he says I'm pregnant....and you know why!"

"Look, Sachiko....I need some time to think...let me call you back...yes, yes, I will, in..in...in another hour... okay...? Please...I need time to think...."

"There's nothing to think about! You have to marry me!" Sachiko sobbed.

"Okay...okay...just give me an hour...I'll call you back...I promise.." Tadao pleaded.

Miyoshi could not hear what Sachiko was saying, only the high-pitched wailing. But she knew it was something very serious. She clenched the dish towel she was holding tightly in her hands.

Still shaking, Tadao took Miyoshi's hand and sat down with her at the table. Miyoshi stared intently at him, waiting for an explanation.

"I...I don't know how to...how to explain this," Tadao, his head sunk in misery, grasped more tightly onto Miyoshi's hand.

"You remember...when you weren't feeling well, and...and Sachiko seemed so depressed about something... so I took her to the waterfall for lunch...? I don't know why...I can't explain...I don't, I didn't want to..."

Miyoshi pulled her hand away from Tadao's grasp. She looked at Tadao, her eyes wide with shock and pain. She could see her worst fears confirmed in the stricken look on his face. Guilt, shame, fear, anger and shock mingled to distort his usually serene features.

"You......and ...Sachiko..." she moaned, but could say no more.

"Yes...but...but it wasn't the way it sounds. I mean, I don't even know how it happened. I didn't want to...but.. well...she...now she says she's pregnant... she wants me to marry her...right away," Tadao said in a groan. 'I can't...I don't care for her at all....I love you Miyoshi-san – no one else."

Miyoshi's face tightened and she drew away from him. She could not bear to look at his face. Keeping her eyes on the table, she said in a very low voice,

"Go now, Tadao. I can't wait another hour for you to call her. Go now, go home and call her and tell her you... will...whatever...But go now. I could not bear it if you stayed here now."

"Miyoshi-san...it was just a momentary thing...she was so sad and she needed me...and..."

"Go now, Tadao," Miyoshi repeated. Her brain was too numb to say anything more. "Go now...go now....go now...."

Tadao got to his feet and stumbled to the door. He could do nothing but obey. Slumped in abject despair, he made his way blindly down the mountain, his eyes misted with tears, a deep sob buried deep in the pit of his stomach.

Miyoshi sat for hours after Tadao left. She sat like a statue, not moving at all as waves of shock ran through her body. When conscious thought came to her, it hit with such a wave of pain that she crumpled to the floor. "I want to die! I want to die…now…I cannot bear this…let me die now," but though the thought kept running through her mind, her body was totally inert, unable to obey any command to move.

CHAPTER NINETEEN

Tadao and Sachiko were rushed into a whirlwind of activity that culminated in their flight to Hawaii. Tadao went through the week in Iwate, meeting Sachiko's parents, preparing for' the trip to Hawaii, in a state of numb disbelief. Sachiko prattled happily about the wedding and honeymoon in Hawaii, but Tadao hardly heard a word she said. He had nothing to say to her, letting her and her mother make all the arrangements.

They were booked in a beautiful resort hotel, one that Sachiko could brag about later. Her father had paid for beautiful new clothes for her in addition to all the other expenses. She put on one of her new dresses, with all its attendant accessories, and got Tadao to walk her to the beach. But Tadao stayed sullen and remote and even the breathtaking views of the beach did not register on his mind. He was in a trance, wondering when he would wake up from this nightmare.

Tadao had been curt and abrupt with her throughout the meetings in Iwate, then on to Tokyo, and finally the flight to Hawaii. It was a package deal, arranged by an agent in Tokyo, where the wedding ceremony was included with the hotel, the airfare and the wedding party – except there was no party. There was only a sad and stricken looking Tadao who went through the motions and said the proper words, but otherwise he had nothing to say to Sachiko. She pouted and sulked and tried cajoling him into a better humor, but in the end, she gave up.

Tadao got very drunk after the wedding ceremony and had to be helped up to their bridal suite. He stumbled onto the bed and seemed to pass out. Sachiko, in utter disgust, pulled off his shoes, but left him as he was. Here she was, in this beautiful spot and she was so alone, so miserable. This was supposed to be a young girl's happiest moment, but Tadao ruined the whole thing. She would give him a piece of her mind when he woke up! She wanted to at least talk to someone, and in desperation, she called her lover in Iwate.

"Where are you...?" he asked. "Why haven't you called me for the last two weeks..? I've been going crazy. I've missed you. You're not mad at me...about something, are you?"

"No. Of course I'm not mad at you. I've just been.... so busy. I'm in Hawaii."

"Hawaii! What are you doing there..?"

"I'm on my honeymoon," Sachiko giggled.

"Stop kidding around. Where are you, anyway? When can I see you again?"

"I'll call you in a few days...let's do something .... really crazy, wild....I miss you, too, but we have to wait a few days," she sighed.

"Okay. But not much longer. I'm getting pretty wild ideas thinking about you..." his voice was seductive and exciting. Sachiko longed to be with him, instead of that sappy Tadao! She sighed again, and went off to the bathroom to soak in the luxurious bath.

She didn't want to get into bed with Tadao lying there, but there was no other place to sleep and she was tired. She pushed him aside, and crawled into bed. Her movement wakened Tadao, and he looked at her with bleary eyes. At first, he could not focus on her features, but he shook his head and tried to see her. With a groan, he realized it was not Miyoshi - that he was in bed with Sachiko. The events of the last week whirled in his brain; the humiliation of his reception by Sachiko's mother, the hurried plans and the ludicrous wedding….all the events piled up and built into a rage. How had he gotten himself into this rotten mess? Just when he had thought he had his life in control, doing something he wanted to do, being so happy with Miyoshi – and then to find himself in this place with this…child. A spoiled, rotten child at that, with none of the refinement of Miyoshi, or the wisdom, the compassion, the warmth and humor…..Thinking of everything he had lost, he cursed his own stupidity. But he remembered how Sachiko had forced herself on him. He had not wanted her at all, but his body had responded to Sachiko's skillful manipulations. So it had all been her idea.

Filled with anger, he turned on Sachiko.

"You seduced me that time by the waterfall," his voice was slurred, but anger had sharpened his mind. "You were the one who wanted me. Well, you got me. So now I can do what I want with you…" he said, in an angry growl.

Delicate as he seemed, he had enormous strength and he pinned Sachiko down as he tore at her "honeymoon special" gown. She scratched at him, trying to pull him off, but was amazed at how strong he was. Now it was scaring her.

"I didn't want you! I never wanted you! I just seduced you to see if I could get you away from Aunt Miyoshi! It was a game for me, a test…and I won! You are just like all men. I can have anyone I want. So why would I pick you?"

Her words were like acid thrown on his face. His eyes narrowed, then he turned away from her in disgust.

Sachiko felt safer now and she pulled herself together primly.

"It's you and Aunt Miyoshi who are disgusting," she spat at him. "You should thank me for getting you away from her! What did you think you were doing anyway? She's old enough to be your mother!"

"You wouldn't understand. It has nothing to do with age. We loved each other….we love…" Tadao could not go on.

"Love her? You must be kidding! Well, but even so, you couldn't marry her! So what were you thinking of…?"

"You wouldn't understand…" was all he could say.

"Well, I still did you a favor! If you want to know the truth, I don't even think this baby is yours. I have a lover who's a real man – he's married now so it was a bit inconvenient for me to get pregnant, and I would have done something about it, but my mother found out I was pregnant and I had to tell her something. So I told her about you, and, well, you know the rest."

Even in his daze, Tadao realized the meaning of her words. Sachiko had merely used him, and he probably had not made her pregnant! He turned coldly to her, now in complete control of himself.

"You've used me for the last time. I'm leaving now and going back to Japan. You can file for divorce as soon as you get back. I don't care what excuse you give your mother. You and your lover can take care of this problem from now on. As soon as you file the divorce papers, send them to my parents' home. I'll see that I sign it. After this, I want nothing more to do with you."

Tadao was still fighting off the effects of all the liquor and Sachiko's searing words, but he managed to pack his few things and leave the hotel. He went to the airport and got a ticket for the first flight he could arrange back to Tokyo. He went through all the motions in a kind of numb fog. It was too soon to sort out all his feelings, if he ever could. But he was rid of Sachiko and her evil manipulations. He knew he could not go back to Miyoshi. It would be too much to ask of her to understand what happened. He had to go out and make his own way, not back in the village with his family, either, but somewhere else. He would go somewhere and work on stone. He remembered that Noguchi had a studio on Shikoku Island. Maybe he could go there and apprentice to Noguchi – or find any kind of a job there. That was the only thing he wanted; no, not wanted. Just what he would do. He would never want anything again. As the monk at the monastery had told him, wanting was what created pain. He would work only in stone and not allow himself to want again.

CHAPTER TWENTY

After Tadao left, Miyoshi moved in a fog, her mind refusing to focus on anything. Slowly, she dragged herself through the days. With Tadao gone, all their plans were a mockery. What need did she have for a loft space to work in? Why did she need the garage space? What did she care about the garden? She locked the garage door, and would not let herself go into the garden. She went back to her desk, trying to find consolation as she had before, in her writing. But the silly romantic novels were lost to her forever.

Instead of writing a novel, she began to write notes – copious notes on things that came to mind. In the beginning, most of it was sadness, hurt, and confusion. There was no beginning or end to the feelings – they circled, they taunted her, they came and went with no rhyme or reason. But she faithfully recorded them,

Gradually, she came to find a light lessening of the pain, though the thought of loquat tea, or using one of Tadao's vases could bring a stab of pain as sharp as a knife. She thought to throw out anything that reminded her of Tadao, yet she found she could not bring herself to do so.

And as she began to enjoy again the feel of the carved stone lantern, the grace of a bamboo vase, the flavor of loquat tea, she found her sadness subsiding and replaced by a warm nostalgia of those happy days.

She began, then, to write about their happy days. How they had found each other, how they had fallen in love. How exciting it had been. How much fun it had been. How much she had learned from him. How he had touched her to her deepest soul.

She didn't write about Sachiko, or bring in the details of why they parted. That was still too painful to contemplate. Only that they had parted. And the pain of losing him. A story of a soul's journey does not need the mundane details of human existence. Such a journey could take place in an instant, and last for a lifetime. Time or place was of no importance. She had been with Saburo for twenty years, with Tadao for less than two. Yet she had lived a full, rich life with Tadao that she could never have imagined with Saburo.

She began to sit on the veranda every morning again, to have her tea, absently gazing at the garden. She had no desire to work in the garden now, and gradually, it began to show signs of neglect. She and Tadao had never actually completed the garden, as no garden is ever "completed". It is an ongoing creation, changing as the seasons change, the trees change color, and the plants complete their yearly cycle of growth. Tadao had indicated the general lines of the garden, an overall plan, but it needed to be implemented and nurtured into shape. Bringing the garden to the full realization of his plan would be a job of many years, even for a young man as hardy as Tadao. For Miyoshi, it would demand all of her time and energy. She would have to decide whether she would simply abandon the whole idea, or dedicate herself to it.

"Should I fix it up again...? Should I just let it all go....If I let it all go back to the way it was....it will be as if Tadao never existed. Tadao is part of that garden. We made it together, it is part of me. And the part of me that is part of Tadao, what we were together is that garden....so how can I let it go...?"

As conflicting thoughts tore her apart, she went on doggedly with her book. It seemed to take a shape of its own, dictating to her from some unknown place. She let herself be a willing vessel and let the words flow. Then, one day, it was finished. With surprise, she realized she had worked on the book for almost a year. She had no conscious thought of a year going by, yet somehow, the time had passed and some of her pain and sorrow had eased. Now she could see what she needed to do. She would send this book to Mr. Akai. Whatever happened to it, it was no longer in her hands. Then, she would dedicate herself to the garden. This would be her life's work, to finish the garden that she and Tadao had started. She had no desire to write any more books about love – any kind of love. Just as old Mr. Hasegawa had made the garden his life's work, she would do the same.

Once she sent the book off to Mr. Akai, she went back to work in the garden. There was the rock garden portion that contained Tadao's lantern, and then the moss garden. There was the stream to be controlled again, so that it was a soft trickle though all the areas of the garden. It would be mostly rock and moss; though the greenery here and there would compliment and enhance the stones and moss. Miyoshi remembered Tadao's plans for the garden and tried faithfully to implement his design. Most of the outlines had been determined, but they needed to be filled in, coaxed into the effect they had in mind.

Now Miyoshi was up early every morning, making the breakfast Tadao had devised for her – brown rice with millet and miso soup. Then off to the garden, nipping buds here, shaping branches there, watering the moss, weeding, tenderly coaxing small groups of wildflowers so they would give a hint of color in season. She became one with the garden, often talking to the stones or moss. She praised them when they looked well, and soothed them when they suffered from the weather. The garden became her child, hers and Tadao's, their creation. It was her job to see that it grew strong, healthy and beautiful. Sometimes, she talked to Tadao, asking him what he thought of this and that. He always seemed to approve. In this way, she spent many years, each year easing her pain a little, so that gradually, she did not feel pain, but began to remember only the pleasure of her time with Tadao. This pleasure and love she poured into the garden.

She never allowed anyone to see the garden. Word got round, from the tradesmen and workers who came to the house now and then, about the extraordinary beauty of her garden. People began to ask if they could see the garden, but she always refused.

Back in the village, Saburo's relatives had no idea what had happened to Tadao. Misae explained to people that Tadao had married a girl from Iwate and was working there, but said no more. Tadao had been very distressed when he returned from Hawaii. He stopped briefly at his mother's house and told his mother to expect some papers, divorce papers, which he wanted sent to him. He said the marriage had been a sham, a trick Sachiko had played on him to get her out of a bad situation. He wanted nothing more to do with her, and did not want to speak of it ever again. He said he had decided to learn sculpture and was going to Shikoku Island, where a famous Japanese-American sculptor, Isamu Noguchi, had a studio. He had left the village almost immediately, and a week later, sent Misae a letter giving his new address.

Apparently, Tadao was working there, but he said no more. He never returned to the village, though he wrote to his mother occasionally.

His letters seemed cheerful enough. He said he was learning so much from Noguchi Sensei, but he was not doing anything of his own. He seemed to have accepted the life he had made and had appeared to have found a kind of peace.

Misae could not even tell Taiko about Tadao. She explained briefly that Tadao had married a young woman from Iwate and it had been a mistake and they were now divorced. Taiko was very curious and tried to get more information, but for once, Misae became stubbornly silent and refused to divulge any more. Taiko finally gave up asking, but had all sorts of wild ideas of what had happened. She concluded that young people today are so completely different from the older generation and there was no telling what they would do next. Instead of Tadao, Taiko talked about how strange Miyoshi had become.

"She always was strange," said Taiko, "I told you so. But who would think she would become so obsessed with that garden! Now I'm sorry I ever told her to fix it!"

"Tadao always said she was such a kind person. She tried to help him, and he always speaks well of her. He says none of us knew her," Misae sighed, "But then, she never let anyone know her."

"And what about that last book Miyoshi wrote...? Did you hear about it?" asked Taiko.

"No. Was it another of her best selling books?"

"No. That's what is so strange. It was completely different from all her other books. I heard that no one really understood it and it didn't sell at all. Maybe that's why she turned to the garden and got so obsessed with that. I guess that's why she never wrote another book. I think that living alone like that was finally too much for her. It was a good thing that Tadao left when he did. Still, it's too bad that marriage didn't work out for Tadao," Taiko added.

"I guess marriage was just not for Tadao," said Misae. She didn't really want to talk about Tadao, not to Taiko. Taiko meant well, but she would never understand someone like Tadao. Neither Misae nor her husband could understand him, so she hardly expected Taiko to understand. Yet there were times when she wanted to talk about Tadao, not wanting anyone to think badly of him.

Misae had accepted the failure of Tadao's marriage, but she felt a great sadness for him. He didn't seem to fit into any traditional pattern of Japanese life. She could only hope that he had found some contentment at last, working with that sculptor. The sculptor was half-Japanese, so he was obviously not the usual Japanese person. Maybe he could understand. He was supposed to be very famous, and Tadao could learn a lot from him. Perhaps Tadao had found a place for himself after all. Misae could only hope that this was so.

CHAPTER TWENTY-ONE

After many years, the glen and its reclusive inhabitant took on a mysterious fascination for people in the area. They made up stories to explain the strange woman's behavior, though no one actually knew her. Only Misae and Taiko actually knew her and they would not talk about her. Since no one was allowed to visit other than select tradespeople, the stories began to take on nuances that changed with each telling and intrigued anyone who heard about it. Miyoshi was said to be a ragged old recluse who had gone rather eccentric since her husband died. Or, she was a famous author who had a mysterious illness so that she was disfigured and did not want anyone to see her face. Or, someone said she had a tragic love affair that affected her so deeply, she had lost her mind. No one could really think of a good reason why a woman would choose to live alone up in the mountains.

Years passed, and Taiko died, never having had a chance to see the garden she had been responsible, in a way, of creating. Misae, too, was getting on in years, and after the death of her husband, she moved in with her eldest son and his family. They still lived in the village, and Misae was busy with three grandchildren. She no longer had any connection to Miyoshi. It came as quite a shock, therefore, when she got word from the grocer who delivered weekly to Miyoshi, that he had found her body.

"It was in the garden, right by a stone lantern. It seems strange…as if she had gone there on purpose when she thought her time had come. She was lying so peacefully, smiling, with a hand on the lantern."

"I guess she was getting on in years…she must have been close to….seventy..? Had she been ill..?" asked Misae.

"No, she was always in good health, I think. She certainly always seemed to be well when I delivered her weekly supplies. She looked much younger than her years so it was hard to guess her age….but I guess she was around seventy…I don't know that she ever had any illness. That's strange, too. I wonder how she knew she was dying? She must have known, for I found this envelope on her kitchen table. There was a note addressed to me, and she asked me to deliver this envelope to you."

The envelope contained instructions for Misae to make the funeral arrangements, since there was no closer relative around. Her instructions were specific in detail, yet very brief. No explanation why Misae had been entrusted with this responsibility, but money had been in the envelope to cover any expenses she would incur. How Misae wished her husband were still alive! She had no one to talk to about this. She knew there was a sister somewhere, but she didn't know where, and didn't know the name. The sister was older and might not even be alive. This was the sister in Iwate, whose daughter had married Tadao in that disastrous marriage. Misae was still bitter about Sachiko, thinking she had somehow ruined Tadao's life and forced him to leave the village. She never knew the real story about Tadao's marriage, but suspected something was very wrong with the whole thing from the beginning. However, she had no idea where Miyoshi's family lived, if any of them were alive. She certainly did not want to try to find Sachiko! She gave up any idea of trying to locate Miyoshi's relatives. She was Saburo's relative and as such, Miyoshi's relative, too. It was her responsibility to see to the burial.

She had the grocer take her up to the glen. She was full of curiosity about this place that everyone talked about. She had arranged for the funeral directors in the village to make arrangements for the funeral, so Miyoshi had been cremated in the usual fashion. There would be no one at the glen, but Misae's instructions were that Miyoshi's ashes were to be scattered in the garden. She also had to see about the final arrangements for all of Miyoshi's belongings. There was still the legal matter of who was to inherit Miyoshi's estate. There had been no instructions about that in the letter the grocer had given her. Perhaps there would be some papers in her house, which would help her decide what to do.

Misae asked the grocer to take her to the house since she felt she could not make the climb up the mountain. Mr. Suzuki talked of Miyoshi as he drove.

"She was different, Mrs. Kanazaki....but she was always very pleasant and polite. People said she was strange, but she wasn't really. I think she must have had some great tragedy in her life. That's why she wanted to be alone. But she loved that garden – it was her whole life, I think. I guess if you don't have a family, it's good to have something that you really love to do. I don't think she was unhappy – she never seemed to be. And she looked very peaceful when I found her. I don't think she suffered at the end."

Misae said she might be a while in the house since she needed to look for some papers. Mr. Suzuki agreed to come back to pick her up later in the afternoon. Misae let herself in with the key that had been in the envelope. The house looked well kept, the kitchen was left immaculately clean, as was the entire house. All of Miyoshi's belongings were neatly put in place.

She looked around until she found a photo of Miyoshi, taken for the cover of one of her books. Putting the photo in a frame she had brought, she placed the photo on the family altar. She found a vase for the flowers she had also brought, and placed it beside the photo. It seemed sad, only this small contribution. There was no one to mourn Miyoshi in spite of the fame she had once had. By rights, there should have been flowers from all her admiring readers. But that had been many years ago. Misae lit some incense, placed her hands together and prayed for the peace of Miyoshi's soul.

With a heavy heart, Misae took the urn with ashes into the garden, looking for the stone lantern that Miyoshi had specified. The ashes were to be scattered around it, according to the instructions. Misae was queasy about the unconventional disposition of the ashes, but it had been Miyoshi's request and she had to honor it. She did it quickly, not stopping to look too closely at the ground, so that she did not notice a small, green kappa doll by the lantern. She lit some more incense before she returned to the house.

She still had to go through the interior of the house to see what to do about the rest of Miyoshi's things. She sighed at the heavy burden put upon her. What was she to do with all this…..? She looked at the desk in the corner and noticed something she had not seen before. Going to Miyoshi's desk, she found in the top drawer, an envelope with her name on it. Miyoshi must have known she was dying, and had left this letter for Misae. It was a private message, not meant to be seen by the grocer or anyone else. It must contain special information meant only for her. Reverently, Misae took the envelope in hand, and held it up in both hands in respect before slitting open the end.

"Misae-san," the letter was addressed. "I know my time is near and I want to ask a large boon of you. I know I have not been much of a relative to you, but I can only hope it is not too much of an imposition to ask you to take on the responsibility for my affairs. As I said in my letter delivered to you by my grocer, Mr. Suzuki, there are sufficient funds to take care of all funeral expenses. As I explained in my instructions, I would like to have my ashes scattered by the stone lantern in the garden. Please use whatever you will need for that purpose.

As for the rest of my belongings I have no family now that my sister is deceased. I have no contact with her children. I had no children so there is no immediate family to leave any bequests. I have had one great pleasure in my life and that is the garden that your son made possible for me. I would like to express my gratitude to him and would like to leave him this house, garden and all my belongings. If he is – no longer alive – or if he refuses my offer, it will all go to you. Forgive me for putting this burden on you. Gratefully, Miyoshi Kanazaki."

Misae's gentle heart wept for Miyoshi. What a sad, lonely life she had had! To think that this garden, which Tadao made for her, was her one great joy. It eased some of her sadness for Miyoshi to think that Tadao had given her something she treasured so much. Under those circumstances, she supposed it was understandable that Miyoshi would want to leave it for him. Still, she had no idea how Tadao would feel about such a bequest.

When Misae returned home, she wrote Tadao a letter. She explained what had happened with Miyoshi, and of her bequest to him. She did not embellish her words, simply stated what Miyoshi had said in her letter. It would be up to Tadao to respond as he saw fit.

Misae's husband had died a few years before, and this was not a situation she wanted to discuss with her son. Though she had not actually shared much of their children's upbringing with her husband, she wished now that she could talk to him about Tadao. Only he would understand this third son she had loved so deeply. She could not ever tell her husband how much this child meant to her, but she suspected he knew. As is the Japanese way, one did not talk about one's feelings, but that did not mean they did not exist. And that did not mean that others did not understand. How she missed now his quiet understanding!

She sighed as she lit incense before the altar bearing the photo of her husband.

"Well, I have done what I had to do. I don't know how Tadao will react to this news. If he does not reject it, it could put him in a very comfortable position. He always did like it up there. Maybe now he will come back," she said to her husband, bowing low over her clasped hands.

CHAPTER TWENTY-TWO

Tadao was in the large shed of Noguchi's studio, cleaning up. As usual, he was doing some menial job. In all the years he had been at the studio, he never thought of what he wanted to do for himself, but had only served Noguchi Sensei in every way he could. He would sometimes work on a bit of stone, or polish some piece Noguchi Sensei made, but he never presumed to be a sculptor. As he had vowed more than fifteen years before, he would not let himself want anything. He was satisfied doing the work at the studio, being useful to Noguchi Sensei, earning enough to take care of his simple needs. Three years earlier, Noguchi Sensei had died and now there was not much reason for him to be at the studio. Yet, he had stayed on, not knowing what else to do. For many years, he could not completely forget Miyoshi, or the things they had shared. But as the years passed, he learned to bury the thoughts so deeply, he now almost never thought of her. Yet he never tried to replace her. He never sought the company of women. Even the ones who came to the studio and expressed interest in him, he put off courteously.

He had lost contact with most people he had known in the past. He wrote occasional letters to his mother, only to reassure her, for he knew she would worry about him if he did not write. She kept him up on most of the news at home, but she never mentioned Miyoshi. When he had returned briefly from his honeymoon in Hawaii, he made it clear he did not wish to talk about Sachiko, or Miyoshi. Something must have happened between him and Miyoshi, but Misae knew better than to press Tadao for an explanation. After he left the village, and went to Shikoku Island to work with Isamu Noguchi, he never once mentioned their names in his letters home.

Only once in all those years, he went home to the village to attend his father's funeral. But he stayed only long enough to do his filial duties and immediately returned to Shikoku. He had been very edgy during that brief visit, fearing that someone might mention Miyoshi. He had almost been holding his breath. But when no one mentioned her name, he felt a great relief and left the village as soon as he could.

Miyoshi's last book had a poor response with readers, unlike her previous books. It had not been reviewed by any major publication, so Tadao never knew she had written another book. Since her readers expected light romances from her, the dark and introspective musing on a tragic love affair did not suit their taste. Gradually, her name became lost among the many passing fads and even the people in the village forgot her. Only the few tradespeople who continued to service her needs thought about her, but they did not feel particularly close to her. They did mention the beauty of her garden, but since no one was allowed to see it, it was also forgotten.

Tadao's father had died five years previously, and he had not gone back to the village since then. When he got a letter from his mother, he took a break during his lunch hour to sit down and read it.

"This is a bit hard to explain," wrote Misae, "but Miyoshi Kanazaki passed away last week. The grocer who delivered to her house found her beside the stone lantern in the garden. She had died from natural causes, the doctor said, probably heart failure. As the closest relative she had left, I took care of her affairs. I found a letter from her, written to me. She explained that she had no family left and that the one thing that had given her so much pleasure was the garden you made for her. So she left you everything – the house, garden and all her estate, in appreciation for giving her the garden. I don't know what you want to do about this, but it is all yours and you can do whatever you wish. She had quite a bit of money in her bank account. I used what I needed for her funeral expenses, but there is still quite a bit left. You would have to come here; to take care of all the papers involved.

She led a very sad life, I think, and that garden meant a lot to her. I am glad to think you were able to bring her some happiness."

Tadao read the words, tears blurring the end of the letter. He had not thought of Miyoshi for so long, but suddenly all the images he had denied came back to him. He could no longer deny how much he had truly loved her. He had to go at once to the house in the glen.

Since Noguchi Sensei had died, Tadao had no real job and had stayed around at the kindness of the manager. He talked to the manager of the studio, explaining that he would be gone indefinitely due to a death in the family. He was not even sure he would be coming back, but he thanked the manager for everything he had done for Tadao, even after Noguchi Sensei died. Whatever happened back at the glen, his time on Shikoku was over.

It did not take him long to get to his village, where he stopped to visit his mother before going up the mountain to Miyoshi's house.

Tadao's mother had been curious about how Tadao would take the news of Miyoshi's death. She knew he had thought very highly of her, but he had deliberately refused to talk of her after he left the village to marry Sachiko. Misae knew that the marriage had been a disastrous mistake even at that time, and Sachiko had very shortly after sent him the divorce papers. Misae was not too surprised, and actually felt relief about the divorce. By Tadao's refusal to say anything more about Sachiko, or Miyoshi, Misae knew something very serious had happened – something that cut Tadao off from his family and friends. But she could never get him to talk about it.

Now, when she tentatively asked Tadao why he thought Miyoshi would leave him everything, his face could not conceal his intense feeling, even if his words were cold and abrupt.

"She had no family, she had no one. I guess I was closest...."

Misae knew better than to question him further.

"I don't want to impose on my brother or you staying here, so I'll be staying up at the glen," Tadao said.

"Yes, of course. Everything is in order there. It's quite well supplied so you should be all right," said Misae. She handed him the keys to the house in the glen and saw him off. She wished she could have gone with him, but knew instinctively that Tadao would want to be alone.

Tadao made the climb up the mountain, slowly giving in to the joy he had always felt in the beauty of the mountains. He felt his body relaxing, his breathing full and effortless as it had always been when he climbed this mountain. As he neared the house, his emotions were in turmoil, yet in complete control on the surface. He noticed the house from afar, looking a bit more rundown than he remembered. But then, it had been more than seventeen years ago. He remembered the first time he had seen the house and how pleased he had been at the proportions and design of it. It was rundown then, too, but he had worked hard to fix it up. From the outside, it seemed as if all those years he had spent with her, and the years after, had never happened. The house was frozen in time. As he entered the house, he almost expected to see Miyoshi as he had the first time, smiling in greeting. He loved the way her face became so soft and radiant when she saw him.

He went slowly through the house, surprised that so little was changed. It brought back her image even more forcefully. Here, they sat zazen; here was the bath where they had first found their love. Here was the kitchen with the window he had enlarged to see the mountain view, where they had had so much fun preparing their meals. He thought he could still smell her scent, a lemony scent from the soap she used. Her presence was so powerful, he had to sit down to keep from shaking.

Then he saw her obotsudan, her family altar. And there was her photo, framed in black and draped with a ribbon. His mother had probably done this for the wake and funeral, he thought. But the sight of her photo, the unrealness of her photographic image, compared to the very strong presence of her in the house finally broke the hold he had maintained so long on his feelings.

He knelt before the altar, tears streaming down his face.

"Why did you send me away?" he sobbed, "Didn't you know I loved only you? Why didn't you let me stay here with you....?"

But there was no answer in that smiling, impersonal face, taken years ago for the cover of one of her books.

He sat for a long time before he was able to rise and light incense for her.

At last, he made his way into the kitchen and made a pot of tea. Putting the tea things on a tray, he took it to the veranda overlooking the garden. As he opened the sliding door, he gasped in surprise. The garden – their garden- it was beautiful beyond anything he had imagined! He felt the beauty, deep inside him, stirring in him a sense of exquisite serenity and harmony. Leaving the veranda, he went down into the garden itself. The pond and waterfall had been completed, but now moss softened the contours of the rocks around it. The trees had been shaped in places, or coaxed into pleasing lines. In some places, sand had been raked around moss covered stones, stones which led the eye to the stone lantern Tadao, had made. It was also now weathered and softened with moss. The garden was so infinitely refined, so powerfully understated, in the best Japanese garden tradition. There was a strong contrast of calmness, giving in to an ecstatic joy from the sheer flow of energy, the chi of the elements. Every time he turned, he came upon a subtle change of scene, perfectly designed to be complete in itself. Every aspect was imbued with the deep love she had poured into it, day after day. It was a masterpiece, polished by years of care beyond anything he had envisioned when he first went to work on the garden. Seventeen years ago, he had only an inkling of her unique sensitivity and artistry. He saw her artistic sensibility in the way she had responded to his work, as crude as it was then. Now, Tadao's years with Noguchi had given him an appreciation of artistry, and he realized with anguish what he had lost in Miyoshi.

    Suddenly, Tadao's eye caught a glimpse of green plastic, so out of place by the lantern. This was, then, her gravesite. As he bent to remove the offensive bit of plastic, he realized it was the kappa doll that he and Miyoshi had played such childlike games hiding from each other. How did the doll end up by the lantern? It looked almost as he had remembered it, not as if it had been out in the garden all these years. It was so out of place in the carefully tended garden…..Had she been thinking of him, still playing their game of hiding the kappa? And then he understood what she was saying to him by leaving the doll. She had given all the love and joy they had shared and left it for him, so that he would know how much she had loved him. His heart heavy with sadness, he took the doll back to the house.

EPILOGUE

Soon after Tadao moved into the glen, people came up to the glen to see the garden they had heard so much about. They had heard the owner had died and perhaps the new person there would show the garden. Reluctantly, Tadao had permitted a gardening magazine to publish photos of the garden. He had the photos taken so that others could appreciate Miyoshi's vision and artistry.

While he was showing the magazine people around the house, he came upon a book – Miyoshi's last book – almost lost in the huge collection of her books. He had only been living there a short time, and had not gone through all of Miyoshi's things. He saw the title, and was surprised. This was not one of her romances that had been so popular. He knew the titles of each of those books. "For Love Of A Garden", was a title he had never seen. Her name and her publishers, were on the cover, as well as the date of publication. He had no idea she had published another book, and full of curiosity about it, he began to red it as soon as the magazine people left.

With a shock, he realized it was their love story, not every detail, but every feeling, every nuance of the first tentative joy of discovery, to the lush sensuality of their awakening, and then to the terrible pain and despair at the end. He relived all those moments with her, sharing her deepest secrets and finally feeling her pain and loss. Now he understood what she was trying to say with her garden – that for all the pain, the love remained and it was the love that created the garden. Now Tadao realized the garden was not meant to be seen by the world. It was Miyoshi's private message for Tadao alone.

After that, he could not allow anyone else to see the garden. Instead, he would dedicate the rest of his life to nurturing her creation.

He felt humbled by the love she had given him, but more, he realized the garden was her way of forgiving him.

"Yes, you hurt me terribly, but you also gave me so much joy. How could I not love you for that?" she seemed to say.

Tadao continued to live in the house and work in the garden, much as Miyoshi had done for so many years. He realized that Miyoshi was the true artist, the one who had created this garden. For the rest of his life, his main devotion would be to the garden. Just as she had done for him, he would nurture the garden for her. This would be the expression of his art – not in stone sculptures, but in a living, breathing, growing garden. Art was in the doing, he realized, and art and love came from the same source, from the heart.

Made in the USA
Charleston, SC
22 February 2014